Rewritten

Rewritten

LAUREN RUNOW

Cover Images © Deposit Photos-soleilc & pashtet8286 and © Adobe Stock-Tomasz Zajda & Viorel Sima
Cover Design © Designed With Grace
Interior design and formatting by

E.M.
TIPPETTS
BOOK DESIGNS

www.emtippettsbookdesigns.com

CrossFit is a registered trademark. Learn more about it or find a local CrossFit at
www.crossfit.com

For Chris
My personal Mr. Ashley

Charlie

The flight home is eleven hours long. I try to sleep on the plane but every time I close my eyes, visions of Jacquelyn pop in my head making me nauseous and my chest so tight I can't breathe. I try to get lost in the in-flight movies while everyone around me sleeps but even the most intriguing movie can't capture my attention now.

How did things get so fucked up? Why did this have to happen now? Am I really just destined to have a shitty life?

Every time I look up I see an attractive flight attendant trying to get my attention from her station. She's tall with sexy curves that make her uniform look more like she's working a strip club rather than a professional uniform. She makes her way toward me, tucking her hair behind her ear with a small smile on her face.

"What's eatin' you up sweetie?" she says leaning on the back of my chair so her cleavage is clearly displayed.

Her southern accent catches me completely off guard. "I'm sorry?" I respond, removing the ear buds from my ears.

"Everyone else is asleep, and yet I see you over here with this look on your face. I thought you might need someone to talk to," she says while placing a hand on my knee.

"Thank you ma'am, but I'm ok."

"Look at you all prim and proper but please, you call me ma'am and I feel like you're talking to my mother. Please, call me Daphne." She holds out her hand for me to shake.

I do, smiling, "Sorry, I'm Charlie."

"Hmm, Charlie," she smiles with the look I've seen in way too many women I've been around but I could care less. "Ok, well if you want to talk, I'll be right over there." She winks at me, turning around and walking back to her station.

I shake my head, putting my earbuds back in. The last thing I need is to be talking to a female I don't know.

I try to go back to watching the movie but keep seeing her watching me; trying to flirt any chance she catches my eye. To say I'm a little frustrated would be an understatement. I pick up my phone and click the iBooks icon, reading the book I recently downloaded, trying to keep my head down, away from her glare.

I must have fallen asleep at some point because Daphne rubbing my leg suggestively awakens me. "Charlie honey, time to wake up. We are almost to San Francisco."

I jump in my seat at the feeling of someone rubbing very closely to my cock. When I look to Daphne, her eyes narrow giving me a sexy, pursed lip look. Fuck me. This chick will not get the hint.

"Ok... thanks," I stutter, shocked by her audacity.

"It's no problem baby, I'd like to wake you up," she says turning around and walking away with a sexy sway in her hips.

I can't help but roll my eyes; thankful the flight is finally over. Once the plane lands, I grab my small bag from the overhead compartment and wait in the long line to get off the plane.

Daphne touches my arm then holds up a piece of paper smiling, "I was serious, anytime you want to talk give me a call."

Even though I want her to back off, I'm not a dick so I try to be nice, giving her a simple smile, lying, "Sorry, but I'm married."

"Oh, my apologies, I didn't see a ring."

I shrug, "I don't need a ring to remind me how much I love her." Though I lied about being married there is no lie to how much I love Allison.

Daphne gives me a sweet smile, "Well, she's a lucky girl," and slips the piece of paper back into her uniform.

Outside the airport, I hail a taxi to take me back to my apartment. As I enter the room everything feels different. I look around and notice just how empty my apartment really is and, more importantly, how empty it makes me feel.

I pick up my phone to Skype Allison. It's ten at night in San Francisco but with the time zone nine hours ahead, it is seven in the morning in Paris.

Allison answers by only clicking the button on and not holding the phone up so I can see her, "Hey, baby."

"Hello... I made it home."

"Oh, good. How was your flight?"

"Long. I miss you already…"

"I miss you, too," her voice fading away.

"Why can I only see the ceiling of the hotel room? Hold your phone up so I can see you."

There's a long pause before she picks up the phone and now I can see why she was avoiding the camera. "Is this better?" she tries to smile.

"Baby, please don't tell me you were crying," I say in agony.

Allison's eyes fill up with tears as she tries to fight it. "I'm sorry."

I interrupt her, there is no reason she should ever be sorry. "No, I'm sorry. I don't ever want to hurt you. To see you like this is killing me."

Allison looks up to the ceiling to try and stop her tears. "Charlie… Ugh, I just…"

I plead, "No, don't say anything. Please. I can't hear you say that."

"No, Charlie, I won't. I love you. Please don't think we're over. That's not what I was about to say. I just don't know. It's all still so new. So complicated," she laughs, "but we're used to complicated, right?"

I smile, thankful for her playful attitude. "Yes, we are. I love you, Allison. Please know that. I need to know that we're ok."

"Charlie, I told you, we're ok. Just give me time," she closes her eyes and I can't help but wonder if she believes what is coming out of her mouth.

I can't think like that though so I try to push the idea out of my head, only focusing on her words, not her body language. We sit in silence, staring at each other through the blurry image displayed on our phones. Thousands of miles apart, having no clue what the fuck is going on.

Allison breaks the silence first, "I'm sorry baby, but I have to go. I have to meet the rest of the crew in just a few minutes."

I take a deep breath, "Ok, I love you."

"I love you, too. Bye baby," she blows a kiss into the phone.

I smile, "Till then…"

After unpacking, I lay down on my bed, turning on the TV trying, again, to lose my train of thought in a movie. After watching two movies I finally doze off during the third one around two in the morning.

I'm looking down a tall ladder that I'm halfway crawled up in the middle of the Golden Gate Bridge. I look down to see cars flying by making my vision blurry and my head sway as I become dizzy and disoriented. I look up and see the very top of the tower swaying slightly in the strong breeze as the fog rolls in.

The fog is getting thicker by the second, making my vision of the steps below me even harder to see. I'm panicking. Suddenly terrified of heights. I can't move up but I can't move down. I take a deep breath, clinching the pole of the ladder, praying that I'll make it down and that everything will be ok.

The fog suddenly starts to clear and I see that I'm only two steps away from the bottom and my mind is completely clear. I have no clue what just happened. How in the hell did I get down so fast?

I hear someone calling my name, so I jump down off the ladder and turn around. Once my feet are on the ground, I look up to see the fog completely disappear, showing a bright and sunny day over the Golden Gate Bridge.

Someone calls my name again and I turn quickly as I recognize the voice. Standing a little ways away, I see my mom and dad walking toward me.

She's carrying something in her arms as she speaks again, "Charlie. Come here. I want to introduce you to your son."

My chest tightens as I place my hand over my heart, trying to ease the sudden clinching. "Mom? Dad?"

"Yes, Charlie, we're here. We're always here. Come here, walk toward us. I want to introduce you to this little angel I have here."

My whole body trembles out of control as I take a step forward. They are ten steps away and with every step my body becomes more secure with my decision and excited for what I'm about to see. When I reach them, I stand, frozen, staring at my mom.

"Look down baby, meet your son, Lyric."

I reach out my hand and softly touch the blanket my mom is holding, moving it out of the way to display a beautiful, blue eyed little boy with soft brown hair.

My eyes fill up with tears and warmth fills my body as I look up from the little boy to my mom's eyes that are filled with tears.

"Do you want to hold your son?"

I take a deep breath, looking back to my son, nodding my head *yes* as I lift my arms, ready to embrace my son. Once he is in my arms, I softly rub his head as Lyric looks up to me, smiling brightly and laughing his baby giggle.

Both my mom and dad smile from ear to ear as they embrace each other, watching me hold my son for the first time.

"He's beautiful, son," my dad says, brimming with pride.

"He's perfect," my mom cries as dad wraps his arms around her tighter.

I look down to my son again then jump up, awakened from my dream by the sound of a car alarm going off outside my open window. Falling back down on my pillow, I turn to the side as tears start to fall down my face.

Morning arrives and I can't get my dream out of my mind. But it's not just the dream, it is the feeling I feel when I think about it. I remember the feeling of holding my son and my heart warms and all of the fear of this entire mess leaves me instantly.

Tilting my head back, I hold my chest, not being able to stop the small smile on my face.

I pick up my phone to Skype Allison to tell her about the dream. It's four in the afternoon in Paris and I hope Allison isn't in the middle of a photo shoot.

"Hey baby, I can't talk right now," she whispers.

"Real quick, I have to tell you about my dream," I plead, excitedly.

I can hear Alex yelling in the background, "Allison, where's my light?"

"Sorry baby, I can't right now. I'll call you later, ok?"

She doesn't wait for my reply and hangs up the phone before I can say anything else. My heart sinks as I click the phone off, lying back in bed before getting up to head to the hospital.

On my way to the hospital I call Diane.

"Charlie?" Diane answers and I can tell she's surprised to see me calling her.

"Yeah, it's me. I flew home last night. I'm heading to the hospital now. Is it too much to ask you to meet me there?" I ask completely empty of emotion.

"Of course, I would be happy to meet you there."

"Thank you," I hang up, turning up the radio that plays Unwritten Law, *Up All Night* as I sing, trying to free my mind of everything that's going on.

When I arrive, Diane is already there, waiting for me in the front waiting room. She's nervously flipping through a magazine, fidgeting and I'm a little shocked to see her so out of sorts. She has always been so calm, poise, royal-like even.

Seeing her, sitting there gnawing on her bottom lip, helps me put things in perspective and see her more as just a normal human being which tugs on my heart strings – for only a second though – then my wall goes right back up with her. We wouldn't be in this mess if she'd just let me quit.

When she finally notices me standing in the doorway, she jumps up, grabs her purse and walks toward me. Once she reaches me I'm glad to see her pause. Just like me, she's not sure how this little meeting should go.

"Charlie, um, hello."

Even though I'm annoyed to see her, I'm also thankful that someone is here with me, so I reach out my arm and hug her gently. "Hello, Diane. It's ok I call you that now right?" I say sarcastically.

Diane laughs, "Very funny, Charlie." She emphasizes Charlie to make a point.

"Ok then. First name basis it is. So where do we go from here?"

"She's just down the hall here. Are you sure you are ready to do this?"

I give her a questioning look and shrug my shoulders, not replying to her but gesturing to move forward.

As we walk toward the room Diane asks, "May I ask how Allison is doing?"

I stop and face her. "Look, Diane, I'm sorry she won't talk to you. I've tried but she's really pissed off. And now this… Can you blame her?"

Diane looks away, ashamed, "No, I guess I can't."

We walk into the room and I'm frozen, not able to move from the sight of Jacquelyn lying there, hooked up to machines. I look at Diane and all I see is pain reflecting from her face.

This is bad.

This is crazy.

No, this is just really fucked up.

Finally able to take a deep breath, I walk through the door entering her room.

A nurse is attending to Jacquelyn and offers to get the doctor for us. Once alone, I sit down on the chair in the corner of the room, placing my head in my hands, just trying to focus on breathing because right now, that seems to be the only thing I have any control over.

The doctor walks in and notices me sitting there. Reaching out his hand he questions, "You must be the father?"

All of the blood drains from my face when I hear him say the word father. After a second I reach out my hand to him, "Yes, I'm Charlie."

"Nice to meet you. I take it Diane has filled you in on our situation?"

"Yes, but please, explain everything to me again. I don't understand. She's in a coma but still alive, and she's pregnant?"

"Ok, well, we have done more tests and research on what we should do with this situation because we were starting to think you weren't going to show up."

"Sorry, I was in Paris. I came as soon as I found out," I interrupt, trying to defend myself so I don't sound like a total deadbeat. I mean, I am the father after all.

"Yes, I'm sorry, I didn't mean to sound insensitive. So, as I was saying, there is a thin line between brain dead, a coma, and, in lack of better terms, a vegetable. Sometimes that line can be so thin that it really is a judgment call on how long a family wants to sit and wait to see what happens naturally. The tests we ran have come back inconclusive but we assume that it's her bodies hormones making it hard to tell what's actually going on. That being said, the pregnancy adds a completely different level to this equation as well. We have found two cases that are similar to this situation. In both cases the fetus was further along but, so far, this little fetus is showing enormous strength. Surprising all of us really. Normally the fetus would self abort but so far everything is looking good."

He looks up at me and I can tell it's only to gauge my reaction. I sit with a blank stare on my face, listening intently.

"So, in one of these cases, they decided to keep the mother alive and once the baby was born, the change in hormones and the natural bodies reaction to birthing the child miraculously brought the mother out of her coma. The other case though, did not have the same luck. Once the baby was born the mother was officially brain dead and died. I know that doesn't help you much but those are the facts. As I'm sure Diane told you, Mrs. Sanders has no next of kin so it is the hospitals position to pull the plug but as I said, the baby adds a different level to this situation. So, as the father, you have to decide whether to keep her alive for the baby and the 50/50 chance she could come out of it or pull the plug and let her and the baby go."

He puts his hand on my shoulder, offering his condolences.

I look at him, even more confused now. "Are you serious? There's a chance she could come out of this?"

"Now, don't get me wrong. That was one case. One, unbelievable case, but yes, there is a chance." He looks at me, giving me a does-that-make-sense look.

I nod, "Thanks Doctor."

"I take it that is the road you want to take? Keep her alive for the chance… Maybe we could have two miracles on our hands," the doctor smiles fondly.

I look to Diane with my eyes open wide. "Um… uh… yeah…" I stutter, not sure what else to say.

"Ok then. We will keep you posted. This has been a really interesting case so far. Who knows, the birth of your child could make world-wide news if Jacquelyn wakes up." He turns to walk out the door leaving us alone.

Diane sits with her hands covering her mouth, in shock once again. She's speechless and stares blankly at me.

"What do I do now?" I say, genuinely asking her opinion.

"Charlie, I am so sorry. I am not sure what you should do. What do you want?"

"Fuck Diane, I don't know. And now there's a chance she might actually wake up?" I turn around throwing my arms in the air.

"Well, what is your situation with my daughter?"

"Situation? Really Diane? I told you, we're together."

"Did you choose to tell her about Jacquelyn?"

I turn around, frustrated, "Choose to tell her? Are you kidding me right now? Of course I told her. We love each other, Diane."

"Ok, so what was her response?"

I drop to the seat again, putting my head back in my hands, "She said it was up to me. How do I know what to do? But now it looks like I don't even have a choice. I can't tell them now, 'No, I don't care about this crazy woman who's pregnant with my child, and now that there's a chance she could live, definitely pull the plug.' Fuck, that would send up red flags everywhere. But," I pause, "I have no other family. This could be my chance. My child..." my voice cracks as I try to fight back tears.

"Has this ever happened before? I mean, to any of your escorts or clients, the pregnancy thing? You've been doing this for how many years now? Something like this has had to have happened..." I'm searching for anything that will help make up my mind.

Diane sits down, tilting her head to the ceiling, sighing deeply.

"What? What is it Diane? What happened?"

"Oh, Charlie," she shakes her head, "shoot, we were able to live the last twenty-five years with only Nichole discovering the truth. I was really hoping she would never know."

"Who are you talking about? Know what?"

Diane hides her face in her hands, shaking her head as tears fall down her face.

"Tell me Diane, what are you talking about? What does Nichole know?"

"Charlie," she pleads, "You have to promise to keep this between us, our little secret. I really do not want Allison to find out the truth."

"What? No Diane, I love Allison, I won't keep anything from her but you need to tell me what's going on."

"Please, she does not need to know," her voice cracking with what sounds like fear.

"Diane, tell me."

Diane looks down, whispering her confession, "Charlie, I am not Allison's birth mother."

"What? What does that mean? Who is? How does she not know that?"

"Oh, Charlie, we were all so young and living a carefree, fabulous life in San Francisco where everyone loved everyone. We thought we were invincible."

"And..."

She takes a deep breath, "Allison's father and I enjoyed a very open, sexual life. We love each other and have never cheated on each other but we would, um, welcome other sexual partners into our lives," she pauses looking around the room at everything but me before she continues.

"A female we would welcome often was my best friend, or whom I thought was my best friend, Robin. Charlie, there is a reason I stress so much about you supplying the condom and always making sure that you discard it by either keeping it with you or flushing it in the restroom."

"Yes, so what did she do?"

"My husband and I never worried about protection when we were making love but when we welcomed other people into our bedroom, Kevin decided he should wear one. Using a condom was so new back then and we never paid attention to them, especially when we were with her. Turns out she was jealous of our life, my life really, and she wanted Kevin for herself. She purposely got pregnant by poking holes in the condom."

"And Allison…?" I ask in disbelief.

"Yes Charlie, Allison was the result of that poked hole."

"So wait, where's Robin? How does Allison not know her birth mom?"

"That was such a horrible time in our lives. We already had Nichole and did not intend on having any other children, especially with someone else."

"So…?"

"Robin was ecstatic as this was exactly what she wanted. Her little plan had worked perfectly. She, of course, made the situation worse and really strained my relationship with Kevin. I accused Kevin of having an affair with her outside of our threesomes. It was not until I found the condom wrapper, randomly, one day under our bed. I noticed it was a different brand than what Kevin would normally purchase. I held it up to show him to accuse him more of a possible affair and that is when I saw the pinholes through it. Then things got turned all upside down. With Robin I mean, Kevin and I were mending our relationship. So, we did the only thing we could back then. We got ready for a baby in our lives and tried to work out how we would work custody with Robin, which was horrible since I was absolutely disgusted with her. I never understood how she could do something like this on purpose."

"Ok, so where's Robin now?"

She sighs again, "Charlie, she had complications and passed away during child birth."

"What?"

"I know. I have always felt regretful that I was happy she passed, she got what she deserved."

I look up, shocked at what just came out of her mouth.

"I know. I am a horrible human being. But it was the truth."

"So then you just raised Allison as your own?"

"Well, yes, she was. Well, she was my husband's. When I first saw her though, I knew it happened for a reason and I loved her just as much as the day I first held Nichole. We decided to never tell her and to live our lives like I was her mother."

"Ok, wait, Nichole and her are what, four years apart? So how does Nichole know? She can't remember something like that being so young."

"Nichole found out the truth when she was thirteen. She needed her birth certificate and mindlessly I told her where they were. When she saw Allison's she saw Robin's name down as her birth mother."

"Wow, so you told her everything?"

"Oh no, how do you explain that to a teenager? She just assumed that Kevin had an affair and I thought it was easier to brush it under the rug and let her believe that. We were trying to teach her about abstinence at the time, not the possibilities of threesomes. Kevin doesn't know she saw the birth certificates. I have regretted leading her to believe Kevin had an affair ever since. I see her with men now and I know she acts elusive with them because of my lies that men cannot be faithful. Then when her only boyfriend cheated on her..." she looks down shaking her head not finishing her thought. "She's never been close with Kevin either. I was just so terrified she would tell Allison. I was willing to do anything to protect our secret."

"So, let me get this straight, you guys had a threesome, this Robin chick got pregnant on purpose, the baby was Allison and you let Nichole believe all these years that your husband cheated on you rather than explain the truth?"

She looks up, ashamed, "Yes..."

"Man, you're a piece of work."

"Charlie, I know. I have made some poor decisions with my life. But this, I cannot tell you how sorry I am."

"You have to tell Allison."

"No! No, Charlie. She already hates me. If she finds out I am not her birth mother she will think she never has to forgive me."

"I can't keep this from her. If you don't tell her, I will."

"Just wait. Please. I *cannot* tell her over the telephone. If she has to find out about this it needs to come from me, and I would prefer that she finds out in person."

"Fuck, Diane, how do I keep this from her?"

"Please, Charlie. She will hate me even more if she hears it from you. If I have to tell her then I promise I will tell her when she is back from Paris."

"You promise? As soon as she arrives back here?"

"Yes, Charlie. I promise," she starts to cry.

I'm so numb from this whole situation that I don't even think to comfort her. I just stare off into space before mumbling as I walk out the door.

Two

Allison

It's one in the afternoon in Paris and I just finished my first show as the lead photographer. Once I'm alone I can't help but jump and up down, excited it went so well. This is exactly what I needed. Something to get my mind off of this baby and what is going to happen with Charlie. I still have no idea. Really, I don't even want to think about it. I'm at that stage where I just want to close my eyes and put my hands over my ears saying, "La, la, la, la, la," like I don't hear or see what's going on. I know I can't do it forever but it's helping me get through the day for now.

Not thinking about the time zone difference, I pick up my phone to Skype Charlie. It's four in the morning in San Francisco and I feel horrible when I hear the sleep in Charlie's voice as he answers. "Hmm, morning love," he says yawning and stretching out his arms.

"Oh, Charlie, I'm so sorry. I forgot you're in a different time zone. Were you asleep?"

"Don't worry about it. I'm always happy to hear from you, no matter what time it is. How is your day going?"

"Oh, Charlie! I just finished my first show as lead photographer!" I'm smiling from ear to ear, jumping up and down.

He laughs, "You're so cute. I'm still trying to get my eyes to focus and all I can see is you jumping up and down with the phone. I love you so much."

I laugh, trying to stand more still. "I love you, too, baby."

"I'm so proud of you. So tell me about it."

"It was amazing. Everything I have ever wanted. I can't wait to upload them. God, I hope Alex is happy with them."

"Stop, of course he will like them. You're amazing and I am so proud of you."

"Thanks, baby."

We pause, staring at each other. Both of us not sure what to say now. The silence fills the air and I feel my eyes closing and my hands wanting to cover my ears again in my *la, la, la, la, la* way so I say, "Ok, I have to get going. I'm sorry for waking you."

"You can wake me whenever you want. Especially when you get back here," he lifts his eyes suggestively.

I can't help but smile, "Ok, lover boy. Not here. I'll call you later. Love you."

"Love you, too."

Charlie

I put my phone back on the nightstand, moving to my stomach, trying to fall back asleep. When I do, I see Allison sitting on a porch swing in a country setting with a little boy wrapped in her arms while she reads him a book. I approach the two of them and they both look up, giving me a warm smile. I look at the boy and see myself looking back at me. Bright blue eyes, soft brown hair and a smile to light up any world.

"Hey, Daddy. Mommy's reading me a book. Come sit next to me," the little boy says with a big smile on his face.

Allison grabs the little boy, pulling him on to her lap, "Come here, Lyric. Sit on Mommy's lap to make room for Daddy."

I sit next to them, wrapping my arm around them both, smiling before leaning in to kiss Allison, just as a car pulls up. Jacquelyn gets out of the car yelling, "Get your hands off my son, you little bitch!"

Sounds of a text message going off awakens me from my dream. Breathing hard, I'm terrified from what I just saw. I look at my phone seeing it's a text from Paul.

> WHAT'S UP BRO? ARE YOU HOME? I THOUGHT I SAW YOU PULLING OUT FROM THE GARAGE YESTERDAY... I'M HEADING OUT FOR A WOD, YOU UP FOR IT?

> **Yeah, got home the other day. Sounds good. I'll meet you out front. Give me 10.**

Paul and I have known each other since I moved to San Francisco. He worked at the same club as me, but after getting the chance of a lifetime, he disappeared for a few years to go to college. He's made a life for himself since he came back here and it's great to see him succeed from where he came from. I was glad that we stayed in touch when he was away at college because now he's really the only true friend I have in San Francisco.

He's the one that hooked me up with my house and actually lives in the same building, living a crazy bachelor life. I introduced him to CrossFit when he returned to the city and we've been working out together ever since, well that is before I took off to Paris.

Paul has an edgier look than me though. He's tall and muscular like me but he's covered in tattoos, with crazy blue eyes, dimples that I watch girls swoon over every time they see them and he's a cocky son-of-a-bitch, which is probably why we always got along so well.

"What's up, bro? How was Paris?" Paul greets me with a handshake dance as we meet out front of our apartment building and start walking toward the gym.

"Really good. Sad to be back."

"Yeah, so what did you do? Was it just for vacation or what? Don't tell me some rich chick paid to take you with her for a couple of weeks?" he laughs and I almost wish that was the case just so I could see the jealous look on his face.

Not many people know what I really do, or did, for a living but I always bragged to Paul about it, loving how jealous he would get and knowing he would never rat me out.

But no, I stop to look at him with a stern face, "I quit."

Paul steps back in shock, "You did what?"

"Yup, I quit. No more. I'm done."

"You have got to be shitting me? Why would you ever do such a thing? Have you gone insane?"

I laugh as we start to walk again, "No man. I met someone, her name's Allison."

Paul stops walking again, dropping his hands to his knees, laughing, "Shut the fuck up. You are not giving up your fabulous life for a girl. Let alone a girl you just met." He hits my arm like he's trying to talk some sense into me.

I throw my head back laughing. "I know, I know. But it's true. I quit." I grab his arm, "But oh, man. Wait till you see her. It's all worth it, if you know what I mean. Wait, you saw her that day I brought her to workout with me."

Paul gives me an are-you-kidding-me look. "That chick? Ok, I'll admit it, she was hot. I even got a small chub watching her stretch."

I hit his arm at his admission making him laugh as he rubs his arm for relief, "But just wait till she's old and fat and not giving you any sex 'cause she's sick of your ass. I'll be the one laughing then. Wait," he grabs my arm this time, "so there's an opening with your madam now I take it?" He lifts his eyebrows to me.

I laugh, hitting him back. "Dream on, they'll never go for your punk ass."

"What, they don't like the bad boy look?" He tries to look as sexy as he can, making me laugh even harder.

I open the door to our CrossFit box, "Come on, I've got some steam I need to blow off."

"Wow. If it isn't the missing Charlie Ashley back from the dead. Where the hell have you been?" Andy screams across the gym as we walk through the door.

"I've been in Paris. Don't worry, I didn't go to another gym, I would never leave you guys."

"Paris, oh-uh-oh, look at you Mr. 'oh I was just in Paris,'" he teases me.

"Yeah, with that hot chick he brought in last month," Paul pipes in.

Andy throws his head back, "Shut up. Man, she was hot. Ok, now I totally hate you. I think it's only fitting that you have to do the 50 burpee, I-haven't-been-coming-to-the-gym, punishment."

Paul laughs, hitting my arm, "That's perfect."

"You know what…" Andy shouts out, "Make it 100, just because you were with her." Then he comes closer to Paul and I, whispering, "I'm assuming you've been doing a ton of cardio workouts so you should be just fine, right?" then laughs, walking away.

Paul laughs, agreeing with Andy, "Shit, he's taking it easy on you. I would have made you do 200 just for quitting your perfect job that every man wants, for a fucking girl."

We both walk to the rower to begin our warm-up. Once finished, Paul walks to set up his WOD and I begin counting down the 100 burpees. Even though the workout totally sucks, it's actually perfect as the monotonous movements help me think about what I will do if Jacquelyn actually does wake up.

Pain by Three Days Grace plays over the speakers talking about pain without love and I'm stuck for a minute, lost in the lyrics. I've been numb for so many years and what they say is so true. Now that I've had my eyes opened to love, I would rather feel this pain I'm feeling now than nothing at all.

Once back at my apartment and showered, I pick up my phone to call Jason.

"Hey, look who's back from Paris," Jason answers the phone as friendly as ever.

"Yup, I'm home. Thinking of heading to Vacaville today. Do you guys have plans? Can I stop by?"

"Man, we never have plans. Just these damn kids," he laughs. "Stop by anytime. USC game is on at noon so try to make it by then and we can watch the game."

"Sounds good. See you then." I grab my things and head out the door.

Fall time is the best weather in San Francisco. It's always a little warmer than the cold weather that is the summer here. I drop the top to the Mustang, knowing it will only get nicer the closer I get to Vacaville.

As I pull up to Jason and Jen's house on the outskirts of Vacaville, Mason and Leighton come running out, tackling me once I'm out of the car.

"Hey buddies!" I wrap my arms around both of them as we all go tumbling onto the ground, laughing that I lost my balance by their attack.

We're all laughing as Jason walks out the front door frustrated with his kids, "Boys! Really?"

I smile, trying to calm him down, "No worries man, I love these little guys."

Jason shakes his head offering his hand to help me up. "Good to see you man. How was Paris?"

"Amazing. Sad to be back."

"Good to hear. You and Allison work everything out or is she sick of your ass already?" he teases.

"We're good, but man, what would my life be without drama?" I give Jason a stern look.

"Shut the fuck up. What now? Here, come in."

We walk into the house and are greeted by Jen who's walking down the hallway.

"Charlie! You're back. Glad to see you." She gives me a big hug. "Where's Allison?"

"He was just about to tell me what's going on with that," Jason answers for me.

"Oh, it's nothing like that. Well, hopefully not," I look down, sticking my hands in my pockets.

"Ok Charlie, what's going on?" Jen tilts her head down trying to look into my eyes just as Mason grabs my arm trying to drag me into his room. I'm not quite ready to spill everything so I smile and follow Mason into his room. "Mason, leave your Uncle Charlie alone."

I look up to her, smiling, "It's ok. I need some Mason time right now."

She shrugs and walks back into the kitchen.

"Ok, well spend all the time you need. We'll enjoy the silence out here," Jason jokes.

Mason pulls me into his room to show me the new guitar song he learned on his electric guitar. I sit back admiring Mason and the little boy he has become. It was my idea for Mason to take guitar lessons when I bought him his first guitar for Christmas and I could not be more proud of his progress.

I show him a few tips and pick up Mason's acoustic guitar to play along with him. Our time together melts my heart as I think of my dreams and my parents saying I had a son. My eyes start to tear up as I put down the guitar and wrap my arms around Mason.

Walking out into their living room, I feel more prepared now to fill Jason and Jen in on what's going on. I stop at their kitchen counter, placing my hands on their black granite countertops that look out to their living room where Jason is watching the USC game.

Jen walks over to me, placing her hands on mine, "So, what's up Charlie?"

I take a deep breath as Jason mutes the game and turns his attention to me. "So, what's the drama now?"

"Man, things couldn't get more screwed up."

"With Allison?" Jen asks.

"No, we had an amazing time in Paris."

"Yeah, I bet you did," Jason laughs and Jen gives him a funny look.

I smirk, "Yeah, it was good," then raise my eyebrows to Jason. "But then I got a call from her mom."

Jen interrupts, "Your madam right?"

"My old madam," I correct her. "Turns out Jacquelyn, the woman that caused all the drama last time, is, I guess you can say, kind of dead."

Jason questions, "How can you be 'kind of dead?'"

"That's the thing…" I take a long, deep breath, "She's pregnant and on life support."

"Shut the fuck up," Jason yells standing up to join us at the kitchen counter.

Jen grabs her mouth in disbelief. "And it's yours?"

"Yes, it's mine. Diane, Allison's mom, thinks she did it on purpose. I was always so careful about wearing condoms and disposing of them but after I tried to quit I ended up going back one last time and I was so fucked up over having to be there that I didn't realize I wasn't wearing a condom until it was too late."

"Wait, you had sex with her, after you had sex with Allison?" Jen steps back, pissed.

"God Jen, don't hate me, too. Believe me, I didn't want to. When I found out Diane was Allison's mom she threatened to tell Allison so I tried to end it with her. I was so confused and scared. You know I have nothing to fall back on. After that one time, though, I knew I couldn't go back. I called her saying I wasn't coming back, and that's when she…"

"Kidnapped her…" Jen finishes my sentence, still in disbelief.

I look down, ashamed, "Yes."

Jason speaks up, "Ok, so what does all of this mean? If she's 'kind of dead,' how is she still pregnant?"

"That's the thing. I guess she has no family so originally it was my decision to keep her on life support for the baby or pull the plug."

"Oh my God," Jen yells out.

I look at her, "I know, right. But now they're saying there's a chance this crazy woman could wake up after giving birth."

"What?" Jason and Jen ask at the same time.

"I know. I can't tell them to pull the plug now. That's a little crazy. I can't tell them 'No, I want this crazy woman dead.' When we spoke they assumed I would want to try to keep her alive. So now what do I do?"

"What do you want?" Jen asks.

"How should I know?"

"Well Charlie, how does this make you feel, the thought of being a dad? And possibly a dad with a crazy woman?" she asks.

My lips form a small smile, "I've always wanted to be a dad. I never thought it would happen though. Not with my lifestyle." I drop my head, "At least not like this. After I met Allison though, I thought that it might actually be a possibility. Now this." I drop my head back in frustration.

"What does she think?" Jen questions.

"She says it's my decision, though, she doesn't know that there's a chance she could wake up, yet."

"So, she would help you raise this baby?" Jen's voice is not hiding her surprise.

"I don't know. It's all so new. She hasn't said she would, but she also hasn't said she wouldn't. She keeps saying we're ok and I'm trying hard to believe her but I just don't know. But now this chance that she could wake up…"

"Man, Charlie… That's a lot to ask of a girl, especially at her age. Especially asking her to share custody with someone who kidnapped her. Shit, I don't know if I could even do that. Believe us though, it's a lot to take on, having kids," Jen admits.

"Fuck, Charlie, I can't stress enough how hard it is," Jason adamantly tries to make his point.

"It is the highest of highs and the lowest of lows," Jen laughs. "Yes, the highs are great. When they give you that smile, or make your heart melt. But then there are the other times that you really just want to die."

Jason jumps in, "That is no joke."

I laugh, "Come on you guys, you sure aren't good at trying to convince me everything will be ok."

"No, don't get me wrong," Jen tries to set things straight. "I wouldn't have it any other way, but no one really told us just how much work this was going to be. I just want to make sure you're fully aware of what you're getting into.

Like I said, the highest of highs and the lowest of lows. But wait, Charlie, you don't have a job… Have you thought about what you will do now?"

I stop to think. "No, not really. Thankfully I was smart, at least when it came to money anyways. I knew I couldn't keep up this lifestyle forever so I have a good amount of cash saved up. I'll be good for a while so I have time to figure that part out. I've been poor and lived out of my car before; I knew I never wanted to be like that again. The only bills I have are my place, phone, cable and PG&E. Then, I can always sell my place to make it last longer, that will give me more money from the equity I have."

"Wow, Charlie. I'm impressed," Jen says and I can tell she's proud of me. At least for this.

"Ugh, but what do I do? How do I end something that is a part of me? Though I don't even think I have a choice now."

"I really don't know. I couldn't do it. But I know people who have. Just know that it's forever. People think only about a cute little baby, but that baby wakes up two to four times a night, then when you finally get sleep, you are chasing them all over the house to make sure they don't kill themselves. Do you know what Leighton's favorite term is now to yell at Mason?" she eyes Jason.

"Hey, come on," Jason interrupts.

"When he's frustrated with Mason, Leighton yells out 'you fucking dumbass.' Thankfully he can't say the words clearly but that is what he's trying to say."

I laugh out loud, looking at Jason, "Really dude…?"

"Hey, sometimes they act like dumbasses. The other day Leighton kicked some kid in the ribs at his daycare for no reason. That's a dumbass move," he tries to defend himself, laughing.

"It's not funny," Jen yells. "But then there is potty training, and making dinner every night, homework and baseball practice or guitar lessons," she looks to me giving me an evil eye when she says guitar lessons.

"Hey, look at how good he's doing. I'm so proud of him."

"Yes, we are, too. I'm glad he's taking them. I'm just saying, it's a lot when you put everything together. As a parent, you're just tired. But then they do something, like play that song they have been practicing so hard, and it makes it all worth it."

I sigh, "I just don't know. I want kids with Allison. Not some random psycho that I barely know."

"I don't know Charlie. I know you, could you have really pulled the plug?"

"You really suck you know that? You tell me all of this on how it sucks to be a parent, yet know that I probably couldn't have pulled the plug," I tease Jen.

"No, that's why you love me," she smiles. "I'm real. No bullshit here. I just love you Charlie. You know whatever you decide we will be here to help. I'd love to have another baby around, one that I can give back when they poop," she laughs hitting my arm.

Looking to Jason I smirk, "How do you put up with her?"

"I ask myself that all the time," he jokes. "But really Charlie, whatever you decide, we'll be here for you."

Three

Dectective O'Brien

I'm sitting in my office, going over my notes for Jacquelyn's case when Jack Sanders, Jacquelyn's ex-husband walks in.

"I hear you wanted to see me?" Jack says as he enters.

I look up, "Ah, Jack Sanders I presume? Please, have a seat."

"Yes, thank you. So what can I do for you?"

"So, you were married to Jacquelyn Sanders?"

"Yes, our divorce was final about a month ago."

"I see," I write that down on my note pad. "So, where were you on August 11th, when she was shot?"

Jack gets defensive, "Hey, I'm not a suspect am I?"

"Just answer the question please."

"Look, this is all pretty stupid. The whole place is wired with security cameras. This should be an open-shut case."

"Yes, we're aware of the cameras but it seems the perpetrator messed with the system and the tapes were removed."

"Really?" Jack says, surprised, "How did they know where they were? They're hidden in a wall… Jacquelyn had that system set up pretty tight. I always felt like I was living in Fort Knox."

"Well," he shrugs, "our guys say the tapes were removed."

"Removed? Oh, wait, no, it streams live, to some cloud somewhere. Jacquelyn always said that the cloud portion couldn't be turned off."

I tilt my head, "Oh, really? And do you know how to access this cloud?"

"Yeah, it's all written down at the house. Look, I have somewhere I have to be but I can go there right now and show you but then I have to go."

"Well," I stand up from my chair, "After you…"

We drive separately to Jacquelyn's house. Once entering the house Jack stops, surprised to see the entry way still splattered with her blood. "Wow, this just got more real…"

I walk by, not affected at all by the scene, "Yeah, since no one lives here we decided to leave the crime scene up in case we needed to come back to it. So where's this system?"

"It all happened right here?" his eyes are big in shock.

"Yup," I say with no emotion. "So, again, where's that alarm system you were going to show me?"

"Um, this way…"

We walk to the study and he presses on a hidden portion of the wall that opens up wide to display an entire closed circuit security system with twelve monitors displaying both portions of inside and outside the house.

"Wow, yeah, we didn't know this system existed."

"Yeah, she had the other system more as a decoy," he pauses shaking his head. "I always thought it was crazy to need two but I guess in the end she was right." He looks down to his watch, "Ok, sorry but I really have to go."

He shows me how to work the system and leaves me alone to watch the tapes.

I press in the system the date of August 11th and start to play the recording. Unfortunately there's no sound so I sit in silence watching for something.

I see Jacquelyn leave and watch more intently for any activity around her property until I see her car pull up again.

That's when I start to watch everything unravel. Jacquelyn reaches in the back of her white Mercedes, pulling a woman out by her hair, yelling at her. I never get a look at her face but can tell she's maybe early twenties, long darker hair that looks like it's about to be ripped out of her head by Jacquelyn pulling so hard.

I sit up in my chair, surprised to see what's going on.

I switch the big screen view to the entryway camera that shows the woman standing with her arms wrapped around herself but her back is to me so I still can't see her face.

Jacquelyn comes back into view with a chair where she forces her to sit down and proceeds to tie her up. *What the fuck?* I watch intently.

I can tell the phone rings and watch as Jacquelyn talks on it, obviously changing her mood and forcing the phone up to the woman before ending the phone call and disappearing from any camera views.

I search all the other cameras but none show where Jacquelyn went. I watch as the woman sits, tied up, alone. Her back is still to the camera and I watch as her body noticeably trembles.

Nothing's happening so I fast-forward the tape twenty minutes or so until I see Jacquelyn come back into view, then a blue older Mustang pulls up out front. A man jumps out of the car and I perk up again, writing down on my note pad the time stamp on the video for reference when someone else arrives.

I watch as Jacquelyn opens the door when he runs up. It's obvious they have a confrontation as he tries to get to the woman. Jacquelyn flashes a gun around and I take more notes, specifically writing who had the gun first.

The man is trying to calm her down when I see another car pull up, a black Audi A6. A woman jumps out of the car, running in through the door. Once I get a good view I see it's Diane Hayes, the woman I met in the hospital who said she found Jacquelyn shot. *Ok, so finding her shot was obviously a lie. What else is she lying about?*

It's obvious that the woman tied up knows Diane because she tries harder to free herself from the ropes that hold her down as she bursts in.

Fuck, I wish there was sound.

I watch as they all talk until the man slowly starts to walk toward Jacquelyn. Something has happened and the mood between all of them has changed. The man approaches Jacquelyn and I jump when I see the man bring her head down to his knee.

They struggle for the gun, and then everyone stops, the man moving back, holding up his arms as Jacquelyn falls to the ground.

Holy shit. I lean in closer to watch as the man runs to the woman, untying her, holding her to him. She's had her back to me the entire time and now her face is tucked into him so I can't get a great look at her, only from the side which does me no good.

It's obvious this man has feelings for this chick. But who is she and who is he? What was Jacquelyn doing and how does Diane fit in all of this?

Diane checks for a pulse, her and the man yelling at each other before he leaves with the woman.

Diane makes a phone call and after she hangs up the phone, I watch her leave one view and pick her up near the sliding glass door in the back. I watch as she breaks the door, setting up the scene, knocking things over, and wiping everything down, including the car and the back seat.

Fuck me… no wonder we didn't find any prints. Ok Diane, what are you hiding and who are these two other people? I shake my head, writing more notes.

When the police arrive on scene I know there's nothing more to see so I start rewinding the footage, trying to get more information to see if either Diane, the woman or the man are at the house any other time.

I don't have to go back far to see that the man was there the day before.

At first I just watch him enter then leave around an hour later. Nothing else appears on any of the screens so I keep rewinding. Seeing him come and go a few more times is frustrating and I'm about to give up when I see them come into view through the backyard camera.

I watch as the man opens the sliding glass door, guiding Jacquelyn, who is naked and blindfolded, outside, proceeding to have sex with her while her arms are handcuffed above her head. My eyes get big as I watch the two of them.

Whoa. This shit is kinky.

Once the man and Jacquelyn go back inside I can't see anything that happens so I hit rewind again to the day before where I see them having sex in the entryway.

Hello.

I rewind it to the beginning to watch their entire encounter. Taking notes on the fact that Jacquelyn ravages him at the front door.

I rewind it as far back as it can go but don't see the man, the woman or Diane any other time. I look over my notes that read:

- Jacquelyn brings woman to house and ties her up. Who is she? Why?
- Man arrives at 12:06. Who is he?
- Diane Hayes arrives at 12:10
- Woman tied up knows Diane Hayes and man
- Mood changes, Jacquelyn puts the gun down
- Man hits Jacquelyn in her nose, they fight over gun. Jacquelyn's shot
- Man unties woman and leaves with her
- Diane calls 911
- Diane damages door – faking break in. Why? What is she hiding?
- Same man is at house multiple times prior to shooting
- They have sex outside and in entryway
- Man must be dad to baby

Four

Allison

Alex and I are sitting in his hotel room looking over my photos from the fashion show. He's quiet, looking at every photo and I'm sick to my stomach, so nervous for his critique.

"Wow, Allison," he finally speaks. "I must say. I'm impressed, though I knew I would be," he winks at me.

"Really, you like them?" I smile brightly.

"Yes, they're wonderful. I know our client will be very happy. Job well done."

"Thank you so much for this opportunity. I loved every second of it."

"We should celebrate. Didn't you say that Charlie had to fly home? Do you have any plans tonight?"

"He did. I don't have any plans, I'd love to celebrate."

Really I'd love anything right now that isn't me sitting in my room, alone, crying my eyes out.

"Great. There's a place I wanted to try before we head back to San Francisco. Say I'll meet you at your room at seven?"

"Ok." I grab my bag and head out of his room.

I pick up my phone to call Charlie to tell him about the photo critique.

"Hello my love," Charlie answers as he's stepping out of the shower, dripping wet.

"Hey sexy."

"Yeah, you like that?" he smiles his cocky smile.

"Oh jeez," I smirk. "Alex just went over all of my photos and loved them!"

"Of course he did baby. You're amazing, I tell you that all the time and he knows it, too."

"He wants to take me to dinner tonight to celebrate."

"Whoa, whoa… Hold up now. He's not trying to hit on you is he?"

Really? Did he just say that?

"Stop, Charlie, it's nothing like that. He just wants to congratulate me on my work."

"Um, no, guys don't take girls out to dinner unless they want something."

"Really, it's nothing. He's my boss, remember." Ugh, now I kind of regret even calling him. Being irritated by Charlie suggesting something so ridiculous is the last thing I need right now.

"I know that, I just hope he remembers that, too."

"Whatever Charlie," I say, rolling my eyes.

"Hey, look, I'm sorry. I'm just upset I'm not there with you. I should be the one taking you to dinner to celebrate."

"We will. I come home on Friday, you can take me out then," I say with very little emotion.

He smirks, "You can bet I'm going to take you but it won't be anywhere out in public."

I'll admit, I'm intrigued by his comment and I can't help but smirk, "Oh really now. And how do you plan on taking me?"

He tilts his head back laughing as a sexy smile comes over his face, "You just wait. I'm going to take you higher than you have ever been before."

"Is that a promise?"

"Ah, this is torture. Can't you come home sooner than Friday?"

"What did you say to me before? Good things come to those who wait."

"Yes, and I'd wait for you forever if I had to."

"Well, good thing you don't have to. I better get going. Love you."

"I love you, too. And I'm serious, pay attention to that boss of yours. Don't let him think he can get in your pants without me there."

"Come on Charlie, you act like just because you aren't here I would even consider it. Give me more credit than that. I promise that he won't, it's not like that, ok. Bye Charlie."

"Till next time my love."

Right at seven there's a knock at the door. Alex stands tall, dressed in black dress slacks and a cashmere sweater with a dress shirt underneath and his sleeves rolled up. "Hello, Allison," he smiles as I open the door.

"Hi, Alex. Man, I'm sorry. I think I'm underdressed." I look down to my skinny jeans with slip on booties and a tight sweater knit top.

"Don't be silly. What you're wearing is fine," Alex smiles.

"Ok good, shall we?"

We head toward the elevator and wait in silence until the doors open. "So, tell me about this restaurant?" I ask as we walk in.

"It's a little place with only tables for two tucked away down a small alley. I heard the food was good but didn't want to go by myself."

"Sounds good."

We walk to the restaurant and are seated at a small table. I'm nervous about what to say. The only time I've spoken with him was in my original interview or while we were actually shooting. This is a totally different setting and as I sit down in my seat I realize I know nothing about this man besides the fact that he's an amazing photographer.

Thankfully, he breaks the ice, "Thank you for stepping in for the photo shoot today. You have no idea how nice it is to know that I can trust someone to take my place when I can't be there. You really did a great job, you should be proud."

He's taking his napkin from the table and folding it in his lap, not looking at me while he speaks which makes me even more nervous. I get the feeling this is going to be a long, very stuffy business dinner instead of a more friendly dinner.

"Thank you for the opportunity. It really means so much to me. I feel like my dreams are coming true."

At that he looks up, his eyes meet mine and I see a look that reminds me of my father. That proud daddy look I get when I tell him about a big accomplishment of mine. Alex's face relaxes and I can tell the mood has changed.

I smile at him and he returns my smile, "I love to hear you say that. You remind me so much of myself when I was your age, full of life, enthusiasm and passion for photography. You really have what it takes to go far. I'm glad you applied for this internship. It's been great having you on my team."

"That means a lot to hear you say that. I know I've said this a ton of times but I really can't thank you enough for this opportunity."

After simple chitchat about photo shoots and the industry as a whole I'm feeling comfortable enough that I ask, "So, how did you get into photography in the first place?"

"Funny story really. My wife and I were high school sweethearts."

I cut him off, a little surprised, "You're married?"

He smirks, "Yes, have been for 25 years... So her dream was to be a model so I offered to take photos of her to help build her portfolio. I had no clue what I was doing and this was before the digital world we live in today so I started with just a simple point and shoot camera. Man, those photos were awful. We both knew it. But I loved her and I really wanted to help her follow her dreams so I went to the library, yes, this was even before the Internet," he laughs, "and I did all the research I could about lighting, aperture, shutter speed, everything. The more I looked into it, the more I really enjoyed what I was reading. I took all my savings and went out to buy a more advanced camera and long story short, here I am today."

"Wow, that is a cool story. So, your wife, how come she's not here, in Paris, I mean?"

"She's at home with our daughter. She's in college and she came home for the summer so she wanted to spend as much time as she could with her. Have their girl time together."

"You have a daughter, too?" I laugh in surprise.

"Yeah, I know, I keep my private life pretty separate from the set but yes, she just turned 21. You remind me so much of her. She's studying film at NYU. This will be her last year. Here," he pulls out his phone, "I'll show you her picture." He swipes on his phone that displays a photo of his wife and daughter as his screen saver.

"Wow, they're both beautiful. They really look alike."

"Yeah, Candace, my wife, really wanted Marissa, my daughter, to follow in her foot steps of modeling but she's never been interested. She's like you in that way. She wants to be in back of the camera, not in front. I was shocked you agreed to be in the photo shoot with Charlie," he tilts his eyebrow, and I know he's remembering how sexy the photo shoot was.

I look down, embarrassed, but not able to hide my smile from the thought. "Well, you didn't really give me a choice did you?"

"Am I really that bad?" His eyes pull together, searching for forgiveness.

I look at him before timidly answering, "Well, I mean… you can be a little intense at times…"

He looks down, "I'm sorry. I know I can be. My wife tells me all the time that I need to be nicer on set. I just get so focused on what I'm trying to accomplish."

"It's ok. You're an amazing photographer and believe me, the end result makes it all worth it. And don't worry, it really wasn't bad, I mean having to take those photos with Charlie." My cheeks grow flush from the thought.

"Yeah, I bet it wasn't. I think everyone's temperature raised a few degrees during that shoot," his eyes narrow as he responds.

The waiter walks up, handing Alex the bill, taking him out of his trance. He pays the bill and we get up to leave.

"So, how long have you and Charlie been dating?" Alex asks as we walk back to the hotel.

"Actually, not very long. Almost two months I guess you could say."

Alex laughs, shocked, "Really? He flew halfway around the world to spend two weeks with you after you had just started dating?"

I stop to think, "Funny, I never thought about it that way, but yes, he did. I guess you could say we got serious pretty fast."

"I'd say so. So, why did he have to go back? Work?"

I frown, "I guess you could say that. He's, um, in the process of changing jobs."

"So, he doesn't have a job?"

I look up, pursing my lips together. "No, I guess right now he doesn't. But he'll do fine. He's not a deadbeat or anything," I say, trying to stand up for Charlie.

"Hey, he can model for me anytime he wants. I already sold some of his photos."

"Really?" I jump to him, grabbing his arm.

"Yes. A few companies honed right in on him. He's got a unique look."

"Yeah," I smile fondly. "He really does."

We enter the elevator together and when we arrive on my floor, Alex stays in the elevator, turning to me, saying, "Well, congratulations again."

"Thank you and thank you so much for dinner. This was nice."

His lips tilt up to a semi-smile, "It was. See you tomorrow."

Five

Allison

I had two more shows to shoot with the rest of the crew before I was able to head home. As I load the plane my stomach starts to do somersaults since I'm not sure if I'm ready to face what awaits me at home. Charlie and I have spoken but not about anything regarding the baby or what he plans on doing.

The only thing I do know is that I don't want how I feel to influence Charlie's decision. That is why I haven't brought it up but yet, neither has he. Now that I'm heading home, there's no way that either of us can avoid it any longer.

My flight is set to land at three in the afternoon and Charlie is picking me up. When I think about seeing him, all my worries melt away. I try to think just about him. His face. His kiss. His touch. Not about anything else.

As I walk through the airport to where Charlie is waiting, a huge smile comes over my face and I start to run past the security gate. I catch a glimpse of Charlie sitting down holding one single red rose looking down at his phone.

He doesn't notice me since I ran in front of everyone so I'm the only person coming down the escalator.

I quietly walk up to him and see that he's flipping through his phone, looking at pictures of me with a big grin on his face and every question I had about us flies out of my mind. I have no doubt that he's the one. He loves me. That's all I need to remember.

"Fancy meeting you here. Are you waiting for someone by chance?" I say hitting his knee with mine and standing so close I can smell his shampoo.

God, that sexy, manly scent almost brings me to my knees.

Charlie looks up, brimming from ear to ear, "Allison!" He jumps up wrapping his arms around me.

"Hey baby," I laugh. "It's so good to see you."

He wraps his fingers through my hair and kisses me long and hard before we both sigh, "Mmmm…" at the same time.

"It's so good to see you," Charlie whispers, looking into my eyes. "My place or yours?"

I smirk, giving him a coquettish smile, "Which place is closer?"

"The hotel across the street," Charlie teases raising one eyebrow.

I hit his stomach laughing, "Your place. I'm not sure how quiet I can be and my sister may be home."

Charlie laughs, "Yeah, I sense screaming in your near future."

"Promise?"

Charlie gives me a sensuous look as we walk to pick up my bags and head for his car.

Charlie starts the car with his phone connected to the stereo and cued up to play Unwritten Law *Love Love Love*. He places his hand on my knee as the song begins. Leaning over, I give him a sweet kiss as we pull out of the parking lot.

The drive feels like it takes forever. His hand keeps inching up my thigh and I laugh, having to move it back down to the safe zone. It's a damn good thing I'm wearing jeans or I know his fingers would have no problem finding their way home before we actually make it home.

As we walk into his apartment I notice three picture frames sitting throughout his place displaying pictures of me alone, or the two of us together. I can't help but smile as I place my purse down on the breakfast bar.

Charlie walks up, putting his hands on my hips from behind, pulling me closer whispering, "God, I missed you," before he turns and kisses me passionately.

I slip my arms around his neck and straight into his hair as we walk to his bedroom with our lips locked on one another.

Charlie pulls away, looking at me silently. There is no need to say anything. I can see everything that needs to be said with the dark passion that has taken over his beautiful blue eyes.

He walks to his dresser to press play on his iPod and an orchestra starts to play through the speakers.

I tilt my head, questioning his choice in music.

His lips form his cocky half smile as he holds up his pointer finger twirling it around as he whispers, "It's Beethoven *Symphony No.3 Eroica*. Trust me. Turn around."

I do as I'm told and he walks up to me from behind, lifting my shirt over my head, then wrapping his arms around my bare stomach and kissing the back of my neck. He starts to sway to the sounds of the violins playing, caressing my body, before leaning down to remove my jeans and panties.

I'm still, frozen to his touch, yearning for him more, getting lost in the intense sounds coming through the iPod.

After taking off his pants and top, he kisses up my leg, turning me around, hugging me tightly and swaying to the music again. We stand wrapped in each other, both naked with not a care in the world.

He slowly turns me around and picks me up, wrapping my legs around him and kisses me softly before running his lips down my neck and walking to the bed.

As he lays me down I instantly arch my back up in need for him, missing his body against mine. I open my legs, thinking he's going to push himself inside but he doesn't.

Instead he slides down, caressing every inch of my body, kissing softly, taking my desire for him higher and even more ravenous.

His touch gets lighter and lighter, to the point where he is barely touching me but still running his lips and fingers over my body, sending an intense sensation straight to in between my legs. I can literally feel every millimeter inside my body that is vacant, the same place that is yearning for him to push inside and fill beyond its capacity.

It's delicious torture and my breathing intensifies as I grab his body, pulling him onto me.

He positions himself over me but doesn't enter inside.

Instead, he licks my neck as I arch my entire body up to him, grabbing his ass trying to pull him into me.

He resists again and I respond by moaning, "I need you inside me."

"I want you in every way. I want it so bad but I want to wait until I can't take it one second longer," he replies while kissing me more, moving from my lips down to my breast, which removes him from in between my legs leaving me with an even bigger emptiness that needs to be filled.

Now.

I grab him, trying to pull him in closer.

He lifts up, grabbing my hands and pulling them above me. Holding onto my wrists underneath his pillow.

Looking into my eyes he whispers, "You are so beautiful. I can't wait to feel you," he leans down to kiss me softly, "all of you. Places only I can go," he kisses me again. "Feel you from deep inside."

I moan deeply against his lips, thrusting my hips up to meet his.

"Tell me you love me," he whispers in my ear.

"I love you, Charlie," I reply through bated breath.

"Do you want me inside you?"

He rubs himself right outside my entrance and I tremble from the pleasure.

"Oh, God, yes. Please, Charlie. I need you." I lift my hips up again, trying to force him inside me while my hands are still held behind me.

"Allison…" He leans down and finally thrusts himself inside.

We both moan at his slow movement as he fills every millimeter I've been dying to have him fill.

The build up was so intense that I'm already higher than I've ever been.

Charlie begins a slow, intense love-making pace while keeping his lips locked on mine, opening his mouth only to breathe and moan as he holds me tight. Continuing to hold my arms above my head.

I'm at his mercy. I am his. In this moment and forever. I know. I am his.

He doesn't change his rhythm or position, and I know we are sharing the same feelings inside without a word having to be said.

I moan deeply as I start to cum and my body is frozen in ecstasy before I start to convulse around his hard cock.

When the waves of pleasure have ripped through my body and I start to come down, Charlie keeps up with the same rhythm and position bringing me right back up to climax again.

I can't help but scream, "Oh my God!" as I start to come down again only to be brought right back up.

Holy mother of God. What is he doing to my body? How is this happening?

He still has a hold of my arms and my body is a slave to him. And like the God that he is, he's taking me to a sexual heaven I didn't even know existed.

I'm completely frozen in shock from the intense orgasm that seems never ending. He brings me higher and higher two more times before I explode so intensely around him that my body can barely even handle the feeling.

Charlie releases at the same time, kissing me even harder, letting go of my hands as he holds on to me tightly.

We lay wrapped in each other's arms, enjoying just holding one another. "I can't tell you how bad I have wanted to hold you for the last week," Charlie admits with a big grin on his face.

"Feeling's mutual. I've never had multiple orgasms that close together."

"Really? Wow, I feel special."

"You should, that was amazing."

Charlie laughs proudly, "Hey, we can do it again anytime you want."

I hop up, straddling him, "Anytime I want…?" I lean down to kiss him.

Charlie laughs, kissing me back before stopping saying, "Ok, maybe not anytime. We have to get up. People will be here soon."

I pout, falling back to the bed, lying on my back. "People? Who's coming over?"

Charlie sits up, putting on his pants as the doorbell rings. "Get dressed, I'll let them in. You might want to fix your hair, too," he laughs.

He shuts his bedroom door as I sigh, not wanting to get up. I can hear a few people talking outside but can't make out what's going on. Reluctantly, I get up and start to pull up my pants when I'm surprised to hear someone burst through the door.

"Allison!" Nichole runs over to give me a hug. "Damn you two. You've only been home for an hour. You waste no time," she laughs.

"Hey, sis. Yay, I'm glad you're here!" We hug once I'm fully dressed.

Nichole laughs patting my hair down, "Here, let's fix this, Dad's out in the living room waiting for you."

I look up surprised, "He is…?" I walk to a mirror to fix my hair. "Ugh, is Mom here, too?"

Nichole grabs me by the back of my shoulders looking at me through the mirror, "Yes, Allison, she is."

"No!" I back up. "Nichole, you don't know what happened but I don't want to see her."

Nichole steps closer, reaching to hold my hand. "Allison, I do know. Everything. You need to come out here. There is something else."

"What? What else could there possibly be?"

Nichole grips my hand tighter, pulling me out to the living room, "Come on."

I reluctantly follow, trying to get my hand out of Nichole's grip.

As we walk out the door, I see my dad first, which makes me smile. My dad and I have always been so close. "Daddy!" I wrap my arms around him.

"It's so good to see you, Allie. I can't wait to hear all about your trip."

"It was great, Daddy. You'll be so proud of me."

"I always have been. My little girl." He puts his hand on my face, giving me that smile that any dad gives when he's proud of his daughter, which makes me even more proud of my accomplishments.

And I am, his little girl. He will always be my Daddy, too. No matter how old I get. Nichole started calling him by his first name, Kevin, years ago. I never understood why but I never will. He'll always be Daddy to me.

I look over and see my mom sitting quietly in the corner and can't help but close my eyes in disgust. "I don't know why you're here. I told you, I don't want anything to do with you."

She stands up, "But Allison, I love you. I'm your mother."

Dad steps in, trying to ease the tension, "Diane, let me handle this." He put his hand up, motioning for her to sit back down. "Allison, why don't we have a seat?"

Charlie motions for us all to move into the living room. He sits down with his arm around me, kissing my cheek as I snuggle up next to him.

"Dad, I'm sorry but you don't know what she did. You need to understand, I love Charlie and what she did is unforgivable. And now we're in this mess with Jacquelyn. It's all her fault."

He sighs deeply, "Allison baby, I do know. I know everything, as does your sister. There is something else that we need to tell you though."

I look at Charlie with a scared look on my face. "What is it Charlie? Have you decided to keep the baby?"

Charlie puts his hand on my knee, "No, Allison, please, just let your dad speak."

I look to my dad who takes a deep breath before speaking. "Allison, now you know the truth. Your mother and I have run a high-end escort service for many years now. I hope you understand why we never wanted to tell you or your sister."

Nichole laughs.

"But there's more. You see, your mother and I have always had a different outlook on sex," he pauses and looks to my mom who puts her head down. "God, this is harder than I thought it would be," he clears his throat. "Your mother and I love each other the same today as we did when we first met." He looks to Charlie smiling, "I hope you and Charlie have found the same love."

Charlie smiles, looking at me, "I know we have."

I smile back, giving him a sweet kiss.

My dad continues, "So, though we never cheated on each other, we would bring other people into our lives, um… into… our bedroom…"

My eyes open widely, "Daddy."

He flushes red, and I know he's embarrassed to be having this conversation with me and I'm just as embarrassed for him. Why would he ever tell me this?

"So, I'm telling you this because I hope it will help with the situation you both are in now."

"I don't get it," I look at Charlie. "What is he talking about?"

Charlie looks at my dad who continues, "Allison, we brought, who we thought was, your mom's best friend into our bedroom. Her name was Robin."

"Dad, I know you had an affair with her."

"No, honey, I told you. I never cheated on your mother." He takes a deep breath, "Condoms were very new back then and we thought they were 100% effective. Turns out she poked holes in the condom to purposely get pregnant."

"What? Are you kidding me? So you didn't have an affair? Wait, are you trying to tell me I have a sister or brother out there somewhere?"

My mom starts to cry. Charlie holds me tighter giving my dad a nod.

"No, Allison, you see, Robin died during child birth."

"Ok, so the baby died. Dad, how does this help us?"

"No, Allison," he grabs my hands. "You were the baby."

What? What did he just say? I'm stunned. My mouth drops open and I'm literally speechless.

Charlie holds me tighter, and I think I feel him kissing my shoulder but I'm not sure. Everything around me is a blur as I take in what was just said.

"So… so…" I look to my mom. Wait, no, she's not my mom, she's just Diane now. "She's not my mother?"

Diane jumps up, "Yes, Allison. I am, I am your mother. I have loved you since the second I saw you and I knew you were the best thing that ever happened to me. To us. I may not have given birth to you but you are my daughter, in every other sense of the word." Tears run down her face as she tries to convince me but I just look away.

"Wait," I turn to Charlie, "when did you find out? How did you not tell me?" I jump up, running into Charlie's bedroom.

I have to get out of this room. I feel the walls closing in on me, and a panic attack starting to take me over.

Charlie grabs my arm to stop me but I pull away and slam the door behind me. Falling on the end of Charlie's bed, I start to cry into my hands.

There's a knock at the door and I see Nichole peek in before opening it further and sitting down next to me, putting her arm around my shoulder, "Allison, I know this is a lot to take in. I can't even imagine what is going through your head right now. But you need to know that Mom really does love you and has always treated you like her own daughter."

I cry even harder, not able to speak.

"You know this took a lot for them to tell us and they did it for a reason. Allison, Mom knows how much you love Charlie, and she wants you to know that it is possible for you to love this child as your own. She has proven that to you your entire life. Yes, Mom and Dad have made some bad choices in their lives but you can't deny that they raised us the best they could and gave us both an amazing, loving upbringing. To be honest, I'm sad I didn't find out earlier the whole truth."

I look to Nichole, questioning her why she wishes she new earlier.

"I found out about your birth mom years ago and Mom lead me to believe that Dad had an affair. That's why I told you he did and that's why I've never trusted men."

I stop her, "Wait, so you knew? How could you not tell me?"

"Allison, I'm sorry. I found out when you were still so young and the more I thought about it, the more I thought it really didn't matter. Mom was always amazing to us and she really was your mom."

"Until now."

Nichole sighs, "Yes, Allison. I'm not going to defend her on that. I agree.

She fucked up. She fucked up big. But she's sorry. She's truly sorry. You have to talk to her."

I put my head in my hands, crying again.

Charlie knocks and enters the room. "Allison, baby. I'm sorry. I didn't want you to hear it from me over the phone. That's why we planned to tell you as soon as we could, in person."

I look over to him, "I know, I'm sorry. I just didn't, I mean…"

Charlie walks over, wrapping his arm around me, "It's ok. You don't have to explain yourself. Please, just don't be mad at me."

"I'm not," I kiss him softly, "I love you."

"I love you, too," he whispers as he touches his forehead to mine. "Can you come out to the living room? Both of your parents are going a little crazy right now."

I let out a sharp laugh, "Yeah…"

We walk hand-in-hand back into the living room. Both of my parents are sitting next to each other, consoling one another. Dad jumps up to hug me, "Oh, Allie, please don't be upset with us. Please know that you were the best thing that ever happened to us. You and your sister. We never wanted you to feel like you weren't wanted or different than Nichole. I hope you will understand that someday."

I hug him tightly, "Ok, Daddy. I love you guys." Then look to my mom, or Diane, I don't know what I'm going to call her yet. I take a deep breath, all I do know is I should say something. "I'm still very upset with you. But thank you. Thank you for treating me like your daughter."

"But you are. You are my daughter." She walks toward me like she's going to hug me.

I step back, holding up my hands. "Just stay there. Just because I thanked you doesn't mean I forgive you."

She puts her head down. I know she's ashamed but I still don't care. I thanked her. She's lucky she got that.

Dad wraps his arms around me again, kissing my head. "We love you, Allie. Please know that. We will leave you guys alone. I'm sure you're tired."

He reaches his arm out to my mom who picks up her purse and walks toward the door with her head down.

Charlie grabs her arm, "Thank you, Diane."

She looks up giving him a small smile, "No, Charlie, thank you."

Nichole grabs her purse, "Ok, I guess I'll head out, too."

"No, Nichole, stay. I miss my sister," I say grabbing her arm.

Nichole looks at Charlie, questioning the idea of her staying.

"Please stay. I'd love to get to know you better. Now that you know the truth maybe you'll stop thinking I'm a douchebag," Charlie laughs.

Nichole smirks, "Hey, I never thought that. I knew there was something though. And look, I was right," she says proudly. "See, I'm a better judge of people than you think." Nichole looks at me laughing, trying to lighten the mood.

I can't help but laugh as I wipe the rest of my tears away.

"Here, I'll cook us dinner," Charlie says as he walks into his kitchen.

"Shut up. You cook?" Nichole asks.

"Yes, he's a great cook actually," I say proudly, walking up to him, kissing him on the cheek. "Thank you, baby."

Charlie leans over giving me a deeper, more passionate kiss.

Nichole clears her throat, "Ok you guys. I'm still here. Hello…?"

We both laugh. "Sorry Nic. Here, I'll open some wine," I reply.

Charlie heads to the kitchen to start dinner while I tell Nichole all about our time in Paris. I tell her about the photo shoots, my birthday surprise, Charlie's modeling with us taking photos together and about my opportunity to be lead photographer during a fashion show.

While Charlie's cooking his text message goes off with a text from a friend of his. He shows it to me with a smirk on his face.

WHAT'S UP BRO? IS YOUR GIRL STILL GONE? I WANT TO GO OUT TO FIND SOME ASS AND I THOUGHT YOU TALKING ALL SWEET ABOUT YOUR GIRL WOULD MAKE ME LOOK GOOD. HA!

Charlie laughs at his friend's smart-ass comment, then looks up to Nichole and back to me, tilting his head, questioning if he should invite him over.

I answer his unasked question, "Maybe. Who is he?"

"Paul. Remember the guy from the gym the first time I took you? He's a good friend of mine who lives in this building, too."

I look to Nichole, raising my eyebrows at her, "With the tattoos…? Oh yeah, he can join us."

"Excuse me," Charlie laughs.

"Hey, I'm only human. I noticed how hot he was," I walk up to him standing at the stove. "He's got nothing on you though, babe." I kiss the back of his neck, pulling his hips back into me. He turns to give me a sweet kiss on the lips.

"Ok, what are you guys talking about? Who's Paul?"

"A friend of mine. He's on his way down. You'll like him," Charlie responds.

Nichole rolls her eyes, "Oh jeez. If I knew I was going to be set up I never would have stayed."

"Come on Nichole, everything in our life was just thrown up in the air and scattered around. Maybe you need this." I say giving her a knowing smile.

"Um, hello, I haven't even seen the guy. Slow your roll, girl," she replies turning around to grab her purse to apply a little lip gloss and I know she's excited from the prospect of a tattooed bad boy coming over.

Six

PAUL

Sitting in my apartment alone was getting old and I had an urge to find me some ass tonight. Ok, I lied. I always have the urge to find me some ass. I thought I would I text Charlie to see if he wanted come along. Charlie's my bro. It sucks, but I can't hang out with my old crew from back in the day because they just want money or something from me. Even though I'm successful as fuck, I don't want to hang out with the suit type of guys that I work with either. It's just not me. Only during the business day can I pull that shit off. At night I go back to who I truly am at heart.

You can take the boy out of the hood, even clean him up, but the hood will always be a part of him.

Charlie's like me. I like to say we are both reformed ghetto. We're both successful at what we do, living the wealthy bachelor dream but deep down, we're cocky sons of bitches who still can't believe we've hit it big. It's nice to share that with my boy. Even though I work for my wealth, he just gets to fuck. Lucky bastard.

I didn't feel like putting forth too much effort and girls always love to hear when a guy is in love so I know hanging out with him tonight will get me in the door with some chicks more easily. Otherwise when two single guys go out, chicks seem to know they only have one mission. Ass.

It takes a minute but he texts back.

> **She got back an hour or so ago. But her sister is here… come on over. I'm making dinner.**

Is she hot?

I plead the fifth.

I'm there.

I look down, checking out my outfit. I had plans of changing if we were going out but my dark jeans and grey buttoned up long sleeve shirt from work today might just work.

It's Friday so I dressed down more than usual for work. If I roll up my sleeves to show off the tattoos that cover my arms it will make it look that much more casual.

Perfect. This no effort night is getting easier and easier. I hop in the elevator and head to Charlie's.

Charlie opens the door, "What's up, bro! Come on in."

"Thanks man. I brought some beer," I hold up the six-pack of Sierra Nevada I brought.

"Cool. You remember Allison, and this is her sister, Nichole," Charlie introduces them. "Girls, this is Paul."

I walk up to Allison shaking her hand, "Nice to see you again." Then walk to Nichole, holding out my hand, "Hey, I'm Paul. Nichole is it?"

I can't help but look her up and down. Holy fuck she is sexy as hell.

Nichole rolls her eyes while she reaches out to shake my hand.

"Ah, a feisty one," I lean in and can't help myself as I smack her ass. "Nice outfit though." I smirk looking down at her high-waisted, short, torn denim shorts that I know if she even just slightly bent over her ass would be hanging out. Put that together with her short black boots, white crop top with a plaid long sleeve shirt left open and I'd be lying if I didn't say I felt my dick twitch just from the sight.

I know her type though. She's looking casual, like she isn't trying to be sexy but she's knows she's a hot piece of ass.

She smiles at my compliment, "I guess you don't look so bad yourself."

"Ah, there we go," I laugh before turning back into the kitchen to talk to Charlie. "So what cha' cookin?"

"Chicken fettuccine alfredo with salad and garlic bread."

"Damn bro, you cook? You've been holding out on me all this time?"

Charlie laughs, "How come everyone is so shocked to learn that I cook?"

Allison butts in, "I think it's cute."

"Cute? I'll give you cute?" he turns to kiss her, picking her so she can wrap her legs around him.

I look at Nichole, lifting my eyebrows up suggestively. Nichole laughs, shaking her head *no*.

I shrug thinking, *not yet at least*. For now I hand her a beer. "You want a beer?"

"Yes, please," she answers and I can tell she's annoyed by Charlie and Allison's display of affection. I feel her pain, too. That shit can be annoying when you're hanging out with couples.

Dinner is served and we all sit around Charlie's small table.

Nichole takes a bite proclaiming, "Damn, Charlie. This is good. You made this from scratch?"

"Of course I did. No cans or jarred sauce here," he says proudly.

Nichole looks to Allison, "No wonder you fell in love so fast. Please don't tell me he fucks good, too. I may hate you."

Allison chokes on her food, shocked at what just came out of her sister's mouth but I'm not. I knew just by her feistiness that she's one to talk like that. I'm just glad my assumption was right.

Allison finally clears her throat and yells at her sister, "Nichole!"

Charlie laughs out loud. "Yeah!" he yells to Nichole then looks at Allison, "Tell her what I did a few hours ago," he lifts one eyebrow provocatively.

Allison hits his arm as she turns bright red, "Oh my God you guys."

I sit back laughing, taking all the different personalities in before saying, "Hell yeah," and clinking my drink with Charlie's.

After dinner we all help clear the plates and I watch Nichole grab her purse. "Thanks again for dinner Charlie. I guess I can officially say you aren't a douchebag," she teases.

"Well, I'm glad I finally have your approval," Charlie laughs back.

I step in, looking to Nichole, "Why would you think he was a douchebag?"

Charlie smirks, "She thought I was married."

"This guy? Man, you have no idea how shocked I was when he said he had a girlfriend." I look to Allison, "Now that I've met you though, I totally see why." I smile a cocky smile at her.

Charlie hits my chest, "Hey, stop hitting on my girl."

I laugh, grabbing my chest before looking at Nichole, "Where are you going?"

"Home," Nichole replies with no emotion.

I walk up to her as smooth as I can, "Well, do you need a ride?"

She shakes her head, "No, I'll take the bus."

"No you won't. I'll give you a ride. Come on." I walk up to Allison to give her a hug goodbye, then slap Charlie's hand while raising my eyebrows up making him laugh. "Thanks for dinner, bro. You know I'm going to be coming over more often now when I am hungry."

"No problem. Just call first," he looks at Allison smiling, "I may have company."

I watch as Nichole gives Allison a hug. "I love you girl. Glad you're home.

I'll see you sometime tomorrow?"

"Yeah, I'll come home and unpack. Have a *safe* ride home," she lifts her eyebrows up when she says safe and I swear I saw Nichole wink at her.

Fuck yeah. It's on.

We walk to the elevator and once inside I hit the top floor, penthouse button along with a code.

"Um, where are we going?" Nichole asks.

I look at her, leaning in closer as I wrap my hand around her tiny hip, "My place. I have to get my phone and my keys."

"Your place? You live in the penthouse?"

I raise one eyebrow up, "Yes I do. Are you impressed?"

She looks away, laughing, "No."

"Oh, you will be. Just wait," I say as cocky as I can.

The elevator door opens right into my enormous apartment that stretches as far as anyone can see.

"What the fuck?" her eyes open wide.

The large room is nothing but floor-to-ceiling windows lining the entire apartment that is bowed to an oval shape. Slate, rectangular tiles line the floor as far as you can see. On the right is a huge sitting room area and to the left is an open kitchen with modern amenities and every high-end appliance you can imagine.

My place is immaculate but nothing compares to the view. I'm on the same side of the building as Charlie but on the top floor so I can see above every other building and even the Golden Gate Bridge is off in the distance. People would pay millions just for the view alone and it's all mine.

"Was I right?" I grab her hand, "Are you impressed now?"

She looks at me smirking. I know she is, she just doesn't want to admit it. "So is this what you do? Bring girls up here to show off everything you have?"

"No, actually, I *never* bring girls here. We always go to their place. I don't want a gold digging whore."

She laughs at my comment but I'm dead serious.

"So what do you do for a living? Or are you some kind of rich kid?" she asks.

"Uh, I'm hurt," I grab my chest. "No, I'm not just some rich kid. I've earned all of this." I grab her waist, pulling her in close to me.

She doesn't push me away and a devilish smile spreads across my face when she replies, "Oh, really. Are you a drug dealer?"

I toss my head back, laughing again. "What, the tattoos tipped you off?"

"Well?"

"No, I'm not a drug dealer. I'm an architect. I designed this entire building."

"Shut up."

"It's true. I've designed buildings all over the world. Mostly high-rise apartments like this." I lean in, kissing her neck. She tilts her head up, allowing my advancement and my cock hardens within seconds. "So is that your deal? You act like a bitch to turn guys on?"

"It worked didn't it?"

"Oh, I like you. We're going to have fun," I kiss her, grabbing her ass and picking her up, wrapping her legs around me.

I push my tongue into her sweet little mouth as I walk her over to the couch. She slips off her shirt, then reaches for mine. After I remove her shorts and my pants I pick her up, carrying her across the living room to my bedroom.

There are no lights on in the apartment but blue light shines in through all the uncovered windows that line the entire apartment lighting the way.

I place her down on my big, dark wooden sleigh bed in the middle of the room, kissing her body as I slip her bra off. Sucking on her right nipple while I pull on the other making Nichole throw her head back while producing the most amazing noise of pleasure. She pulls hard on my hair and wraps her legs around my lower waist.

"Fuck doll. You are so fucking hot," I say vehemently.

"Just wait till you fuck me."

I rise up, shocked by her audacity. Shaking my head, "Girl, you are too much. I think we're made for each other," I joke. "Stay here."

Stepping away from her is torture right now but there is no way I'm fucking her without a jimmy.

"Where are you going?" she asks and I see in her eyes she's pissed I pulled away, too.

"My wallet is out in the living room. I need a condom."

"You don't have one in your nightstand?" she looks to the side of the bed.

I lean in to kiss her, "No, I told you. I don't bring girls here. I guess you're an exception."

Her lips form a small smile.

"Now don't fuck it up," I slap her ass. "I'll be right back."

My wallet is sitting on the kitchen counter next to my phone. Shifting through the bi-fold to grab a condom I see my phone screen light up showing a call from Beth.

Clinching my jaw, I reach down, hit ignore on the call and quickly power the phone down. Tilting my head back, I take a deep breath to rid the memory of the call and turn with renewed determination to the bedroom. There's a fucking hot chick, waiting for my hard cock in my bed of all places and nothing is going to fuck this up.

Standing in the doorway, I eye Nichole laying on the bed with a shit-eating grin on my face while I hold up the condom. "Now tell me, oh-outspoken-one, how do you want me to fuck you?"

She smirks as she slowly lifts from the bed and struts over to me, "I may be a bitch outside, but I want nothing more than for you to take control of me and fuck me like the bad girl I am when we're in here, alone."

My eyes narrow as a smirk grows over my face, "As you wish."

I push her down on the bed and she giggles in excitement.

"Yeah, boy."

I rip her thin, lace panties off of her, "Oops, I hope you didn't like those?"

"I'd rather go without anyway. Easier access," she smirks.

My eyes literally roll back in my head in ecstasy as my dick gets rock fucking hard. And when I thought I was over the edge turned on, she jumps up to lick my cock from base to tip.

Oh. My. Fucking. God.

Who is this chick?

I'm in fucking love.

Ok, not really but holy shit. This is the hottest fucking moment I've had in awhile. And with everything going on in my life right now it's fucking perfect.

She continues her tongue dance around me before running her hands up and down my length.

"Fuck me," I whisper through clenched teeth.

"Yeah," she replies through licks, "is that what you want?"

I grab her head with both hands, pulling her up, kissing her before pushing her back on the bed and slipping the condom on. I want to fuck her and I want to fuck her now.

"Turn around, lay on your stomach."

Nichole smiles and does as she's told which turns me on that much more.

"Tilt your ass up." And damn, what an ass. It's exactly what I needed tonight.

She does and I slip inside her slowly before pushing harder and harder with every thrust.

"Oh yes, fuck yes," she cries out.

I grab both of her arms and hold them behind her back, pounding harder and faster inside.

Nichole screams in pleasure as I slow my pace, savoring the feeling while letting go of her arms and wrapping my hand around her hair.

I lean in to whisper in her ear as I pull her head back, "Yeah, you like me fucking you?"

"Yes, please, harder. Fuck me harder."

"Oh no, you've been a bad girl," I smirk as I pull out and I'm not going to lie. I instantly feel the need to be back inside her. "Get on all fours and grab the back of my bed."

She does as she's told and I slam back into her, pumping faster and faster before leaning over to pull on her nipples, making her sing out in pleasure.

"Turn around. Climb on top of me. I want to see you cum," I whisper in her ear.

I lay down on my back and she mounts me with ease, holding onto the back of the bed as she bounces up and down before sliding her hips back and forth, rubbing herself against me, bringing herself higher and higher as I just lay there, letting her do as she pleases and loving every fucking second of it.

"I want to see you cum," I say grabbing her hips, pounding into her harder, bringing her higher and higher before she screams as she convulses around me.

The sight alone makes me cum, as I tighten my face and grunt through my teeth. Nichole falls on top of me, still trying to catch her breath.

After a few moments, I wrap my arms around her bare ass and smack it, hard. "Fuck yeah, that was hot."

Nichole laughs as she lifts up, flipping her hair to the back, "Uh, not too bad," she says matter-of-factly.

I laugh, "Not-too-bad-my-ass." I lift her up and flip her to her back, lying on top of her. Nichole just laughs. "Don't temp me to fuck you again."

"Is that a promise?" she teases.

"Fuck, I may love you," I say, obviously kidding.

I sit up and walk to the bathroom to get rid of the condom. When I return, the room is empty. Nichole has walked into the living room where she's looking for her clothes.

"Where do you think you're going?"

"Home," she answers without a beat.

"Damn, just wham-bam-thank-you-ma'am, huh?"

Nichole laughs, "Well, yeah. It was good though. Thank you," she reaches up to kiss my cheek.

"Um, no, you need to stay. I told you, I might not be done with you yet."

"Oh, really. And if I leave?"

"I won't let you. It's too late to ride the bus by yourself and I'm not going to drive you."

"Really, I'm a big girl. I can handle myself."

"Yes, and you just proved that to me. But no, I'm not letting you leave, looking like that, with no panties on, by yourself. Sorry, not happening," I say, pulling her hand back to my bedroom.

"Look, I don't stay the night. Sort of a rule. Sorry. Don't take it personal."

"Well good. I've never had a girl stay the night so we're breaking all kinds of rules tonight," I look behind me at her. "Get over it and take those shorts back off. Don't let anything go to your head though. I'll lend you a shirt to sleep in. If you sleep in nothing but that short shirt I won't be able to get any sleep and I have a meeting in the morning."

Nichole laughs, giving into my proposal to stay the night. I'm shocked too that I'm asking her to stay but what the hell. It's only a night.

"Here, I just bought a new toothbrush, you can use it."

"Ok, not only am I staying the night, but now I have my own toothbrush here?"

I laugh, "You can throw it away when you leave tomorrow. Sorry if I care about your oral health."

She smirks, grabbing the toothbrush out of my hand, "Yeah, you liked my other oral, too."

I smack her ass as she walks to the bathroom, "That's right."

After she brushes her teeth she slips on an old, blue t-shirt that I set out for her. It falls just past her ass and I can't help but smirk at how hot she looks in it.

We climb into my bed and I turn to her, teasing, "Now, don't try to cuddle or anything. You're just here to sleep."

She hits me before turning her back to me.

I lean over, kissing her cheek, "Oh, that ass…" I wrap my hand around her.

She laughs at me, smacking my hand away from her sexy little body. "Hands to yourself."

Even though it's Saturday, I have to get up early for work and Nichole sleeps right through me getting ready. She lies fast asleep, wearing only my t-shirt with the sheet wrapped up in her long legs and it takes every ounce of my self control to not attack her and screw her all morning long.

I slide in next to her, whispering in her ear, "Morning sexy."

Nichole jumps up like I frightened her. I smile since she must have slept so good she forgot where she was.

Once she has her bearings she smiles, "Oh yeah, morning." She wipes her eyes and I can't help but lean down to kiss her lips before pulling back and walking across the room.

"Wow. You look hot," she says once she notices how I'm dressed.

I turn around, smiling my cocky smile, "Yeah, you like?"

I hold out my arms to the side, showing off the dark silver Hugo Boss slim fitting suit I'm wearing with a white shirt underneath and the top two buttons left undone.

"I have to go to work, I have an early meeting. Come on, I've got to get going so I can take you home."

"You… you look so different," she says surprised.

"You say that like it's a bad thing."

"Oh no, no, it's not bad," she smiles. "So, you really are an architect?"

I laugh, "Um, yeah. Did you think I was lying last night?"

"No, I just couldn't picture it," she looks me up and down. "I can see it now though."

I grab her ass smiling. "How I'd love to fuck you again right now. But we have to go. Come on. Keep the shirt. It looks good on you."

She slips on her shorts and grabs her purse from the living room before I hand her a motorcycle helmet. "Here, you can carry this down."

"Shut up. You drive a motorcycle, too? You have this bad boy thing down. Well, except for this whole suit thing. That's just damn sexy."

I grab her, pulling her in close, "Seeing you do the walk-of-shame wearing my t-shirt is sexy as hell." I kiss her, leaning her back before grabbing her ass again, "Let's go."

We hop on my all black Ducati and drive to her place. After I park, we hop off and I walk her to her door. "So, can I get your number?"

"Um, no."

My eyes must have gone big with surprise because she laughed before saying, "How about you stop by at ten tonight? I'll let you fuck me again."

"Not till ten? How about I take you for drinks first?"

"That's not necessary," she kisses me quickly and unlocks her door, blowing me a kiss as she shuts the door behind her.

Seven

Allison

The sun breaking through the early morning fog shines through Charlie's bedroom window waking us up. Charlie leans over, wrapping his arms around me, "Morning, baby."

"Mmm, good morning," I say snuggling into his chest.

"Can we stay like this all day?"

"I have no plans," I look up, smiling sweetly to him.

He kisses my forehead, holding on tightly as we cuddle in silence, dozing in and out of sleep.

After awhile I stretch my arms up, "I guess I should get up. I have to go home and do some unpacking."

"I cleared out some space in my drawers and closet for you if you want to unpack here."

I look up at him, a little surprised, "Now Charlie, are you asking me to move in with you?"

He kisses me sweetly, "Maybe…"

I look down, putting my head back on his chest, not sure what to say. *Wow, should I? I mean, I do want to be with him and we did so well in Paris together. But living together? And this baby…? Can I do this? Will he keep it?*

I take a deep breath, letting it out slowly.

"What is it Allison? Do you not want to move in here? I'm sorry, I just thought…"

I interrupt him, "No, Charlie, it's not that. I mean, yes, the thought sounds great but…"

"I'm sorry. It's too soon. Forget I mentioned it." He gets up quickly, embarrassed from the situation.

I grab his arm, "Charlie, it's not that. We just have a lot to work through right now. Have you decided what you're going to do?" I look down as I whisper, "I mean, with the baby?"

"Allison, the only thing on my mind right now is you. I need to make sure we're ok. You say the word and I'll pull the plug if it means I'll lose you."

"Charlie," I snap at him, "Don't you dare say that. Don't put this on me. This is a baby. A life. I can't be the deciding factor in this. What do you want?"

He sits down, exasperated, looking away from me, "I don't know. I keep having these dreams."

"Yeah, about what?"

"About you. About the baby. About my parents."

"And…?"

"Allison, I need to know I won't lose you."

"Charlie," I take a deep breath, trying not to go there again, "tell me about the dreams."

He sits forward, staring blankly at the wall, "The first one was crazy. I was on one of the towers of the Golden Gate Bridge. I just remember being terrified because I was so high up and it was so foggy, I couldn't see anything to get down. Then, all of the sudden, I was securely on the ground and my parents walked up, holding a baby and I had this feeling like I knew everything was going to be ok."

I look at him, trying to hide the anxiety I feel about his dream and the entire situation. "Did they say anything?"

"Yes," he looks down, still not able to look me in the eye as he talks about his dream. "They asked if I wanted to meet my son. They said his name was Lyric."

I inhale sharply at the sound of the baby's name but don't dare say a word.

"Then the other dream was of you and a little boy. You were reading to him, sitting on a porch swing at a house in the country. You called the little boy Lyric as well and he called you Mommy."

He looks at me and I can tell it's more to gauge my reaction from the *Mommy* comment rather than to see if I have something to say in response.

I look down as tears fill my eyes that I can't fight back.

Charlie reaches his arms around me, "Please don't cry, Allison. I'm so sorry. What can I do? I need to make this all ok."

"Charlie, you need to decide what you want."

"I told you, I know what I want. I want you. I want us."

"Then baby, you need to follow your heart."

He pauses, grabbing my hands, "What are you saying?"

"I don't know what I'm saying, but I feel that you know the answer in your heart. I've always been a firm believer that everything happens for a reason and that there are signs everywhere. And these dreams, they are your signs. If we're meant to be together, then we will be. It may take time. And please, you need to give me that time. But if we're meant to be each other's forever, then we will be."

"Oh, Allison," he wraps his arms around me. "That's all I needed to hear. I know we can make it through this."

I hug him back, looking up to the ceiling. *God I hope we can make it through this… I hope I can do this…*

I meant everything I said and now I just have to let whatever happens, happen.

We lounge around the rest of the day, wrapped up in each other, watching movies and being lazy. Charlie gets up to play a new song for me that completely melts my heart with the lyrics talking about his years of tears but it all making sense now that they are together and he just wants to waste time with her.

"Oh Charlie, I love this song. I've never heard it but his voice sounds familiar."

"Yeah, it's Adam Gontier, he split from Three Days Grace and started another band called Saint Asonia. This song is called *Waste My Time*. It reminded me so much of me, of you, of us."

I lean over, kissing him softly as my phone rings with a call from Sonia and I can't help but jump up and down at the sight.

"Yay! Sonia, how are you?"

"Hey girl. I miss you. I just got off work, any chance you can come downtown for an early dinner?"

"Yes, I have so much to tell you. That's perfect. And I'm already downtown, at Charlie's place. I can meet you in a half hour?"

"Perfect. Does our usual, One Market, sound good?"

"Yes. Anything sounds good. I got so sick of the food there," I laugh. "See you in a few."

I turn to Charlie who is lying on the bed now. "Do you mind if I go meet Sonia for dinner?"

"Of course not, why would I mind? You'll come back here though right?" he lifts one eyebrow up, suggestively.

I smile, leaning in to kiss him. "Of course I will. I live here now, don't I?" I smirk as I turn away with a sexy sway to my hips.

Charlie jumps up, grabbing my hips and swinging me around. "Yeah you do. I can't tell you how happy that makes me."

His lips surround mine as I reach into his hair pulling hard before breaking our kiss and pushing him away. "Sorry babe, I have to go. Keep that thought for when I get back though."

I quickly touch up my makeup, grab my purse, and give Charlie one more kiss before walking out the door. The restaurant is walking distance from Charlie's place so it doesn't take me long to get there.

When I see Sonia walking up at the same time tears well up in my eyes as I run to hug her. "I've missed you so much. How have you been?"

"I've missed you, too. Why the tears though, girl?"

I wipe my eyes. "I have so much to fill you in on," my tears really start to flow now. "God," I look up, trying to stop them, "just seeing you, it made everything I've kept in come out in one second."

"Whoa, Allison, are you ok? What's going on?"

"Come on, let's go inside. We need to sit first."

We walk in and find a table and before we're even seated Sonia pries for more information, "Ok, spill it. Are you ok?"

I take a deep breath and tell Sonia everything. Starting with my horrid kidnapping, my mother, Charlie and the baby. This is the first time I've been able to tell anyone and getting the words out makes me, surprisingly, feel much better.

Sonia sits in shock as I continue my story.

When I'm finished, she sighs, "Goddamn girl. This is insane. I knew something was up before when we all went out to Ruby Skye. How come you didn't tell me?"

"I knew you knew, and thank you for not pushing me to tell you. I'm sorry. It was just too crazy. Can you believe my mom? Oh shit," I drop my head back. "There's more."

"Are you kidding me? What else could there be?"

"Ugh," I look up again, starting to cry, "My parents, well, turns out my dad didn't have an affair like we always thought he did."

"Wait, he didn't? So why did you guys always think he did?"

I take a deep breath, "Turns out they were having threesomes, the two of them with my mom's best friend and I guess she got pregnant on purpose."

"No way. So you have another sister or brother somewhere?"

"No, Sonia. I was that baby."

"Wait, what?!"

"Yeah, turns out my mom, is not my birth mom. My birth mom died during my birth."

"Holy shit! Wait, whoa, this is crazy."

"I know. So they just raised me like my mom was my birth mom, hoping I would never find out. Turns out Nichole found out years ago and my mom lead her to believe it was from an affair, instead of explaining the threesome thing."

Sonia laughs, "Damn, your parents are freaks."

"Oh, God, gross, please don't make me think of my parents like that."

"So wait, your parents had a threesome. The other woman got pregnant but died during childbirth, and now, there is this chick in the hospital, basically dead and pregnant with Charlie's baby..." she tilts her head to the side. "Now that's just weird. That's crazy it's such a similar situation."

"Yeah, that's why they told me. Hoping it would help somehow."

"So is Charlie going to keep the baby? Would you stay with him?"

"God. That's another thing. You know I'm all about everything happening for a reason and there are signs everywhere, right?"

"Of course, you have always been like that."

"Yeah, so... Guess what Charlie has had two dreams about since finding out about the pregnancy?"

"What?"

"That he has a boy and, get this, named Lyric."

"Shut the fuck up. Allison, that's what you've always said you would name your son if you had one."

I drop my head back, "I know."

"Does Charlie know that?"

"No, I've never told him. When he told me about the dream and the name I about died. I couldn't tell him though. I'm just not sure. How can I raise a kid that's not mine? And what if we have another kid together? Will I love them the same?"

"Jeez, Allison," she shakes her head. "Damn, that's something only you can decide. But I'll tell you this. If you do decide to raise this child and stay with Charlie, you have to treat that child like your own. Love it the same way you would your own child. Otherwise you will fuck that kid up. It's not the kid's fault who his birth mom is. It will become you." She pauses, "Just like your mom did. She never treated you and Nichole differently. You have to treat it the same way. Do you think you can?"

"I just don't know," I start to cry again.

"Allison, I've known you for years. I love you like you were my real sister and I say this with all the love and support in my heart, but I think you can do it. You love my daughter like she's your own. I've never seen you fall so fast for someone and everything is falling into place for you two. In the most weird, fucked up way I have ever seen, but if you look at the big picture, it's all there. Every sign you need. You found him to help get him out of his lifestyle, so you could learn the truth about your mom, so you can help raise this child. Him having a dream about the baby being named Lyric is just the icing on the cake with a big, fat, red cherry on top."

I look at her, tears running down my face.

"I'm here for you girl. Whatever you decide. You know I love you."

"I know. Thank you. I do know one thing for sure though," I look around for our waiter, "I need a drink."

Sonia laughs, agreeing with me as we flag down our waiter.

We visit for a few hours, laughing and crying like best friends do. I'm so thankful for the normalness that Sonia seems to always bring back to my life, no matter what situation we are in.

Charlie texts me around nine:

Hey, Baby. I hope you are having a great time. Do you want me to come down to meet you so you don't have to walk home alone? No rush, just wanted to offer.

I smile, showing Sonia the text. "He's so sweet. I really do love him."

Sonia smiles, "I know you do. Besides everything that has happened, I'm glad you found each other. Have him come down. I'd love to get to know him better."

I smile, texting back:

Sure! Come down, you can have a drink with us.

Sounds good. Be right there.

A little while later he walks into the restaurant and slides next to me in the booth, giving me a sweet kiss hello.

"Hey baby! You remember Sonia…" I introduce them again.

"Of course. Nice to see you again." They shake hands and Charlie's face blushes like he's embarrassed all of the sudden. "I take it you told her everything," he looks down.

"Yes, the good, the bad and the ugly," Sonia laughs. "But hey, if she loves you, I love you. Don't worry about it. I don't judge."

Charlie looks at me with a slight frown.

"Hey, I mean it. Even with all this fucked up stuff going on, I've never seen her as happy as when she talks about you or the way she lit up when you walked in through the door right now. To me, that's all that matters," Sonia reassures him. "But don't get me wrong, if you hurt her I will personally kick your ass," she says jokingly but as serious as she can.

I laugh and Charlie shakes his head, "You have a deal. I would let you kick my ass." He leans over to kiss me again. "Because I would never do anything to hurt her."

Eight

PAUL

It's 10:20 at night. I'm a little late but I couldn't show how desperate I was to see Nichole again and show up right at ten, even though I've been sitting around the corner on my bike just waiting.

Nichole opens the door wearing nothing but a long, white tight tank top with black, lace, ass cheek showing panties.

Holy, fuck, she is so sexy.

"You're late," she protests.

"You're hot! Do you always answer the door like that?"

"I thought you weren't coming so I started the party without you." She turns to walk back up the stairs, showing her ass poking through her panties and suddenly I can barely walk up the stairs my cock is so hard.

I drop my helmet as I lean forward to grab her, "I wouldn't miss this for the world."

We walk into her room and I see she wasn't kidding. Sitting on her bed is a dildo and porn plays on the TV. Damn, I haven't been able to get this girl out of my head all day and now I see why. She may just be my dream come true.

"Holy shit," I grab her, bringing her in closer, rubbing my hard cock against her. "You weren't kidding. No need for that anymore. It can't make you cum like I can."

Nichole laughs, "Um, yes it can."

"Well, not tonight." I pull her shirt up over her head then wrap my hands around her ass, pulling her in even closer.

"We'll see," she challenges me and it's fucking on.

I laugh, throwing her down on the bed. "Damn doll, you are too much." I kick off my shoes and pull off my shirt. "But I accept your challenge. I hope you don't mind but I'm in a rough kind of mood."

Nichole raises her eyebrows, "What do you have in mind?"

"Fuck, it's more like what *don't* I have in my mind when it comes to you."

"Well, here I am baby. Do with me as you wish."

My eyes grow dark and narrow, as lust filled as I can get. My entire demeanor changes as I turn to shut the door and lock it, before turning to her and flipping the TV off, then the light.

I walk up to her, leaning down, whispering, "How rough do you like it?"

Nichole looks up, bites her lower lip and I'm shocked she doesn't respond. She's nervous and it just fuels me even more.

"You let me know if it's too much. 'Cause doll, I'm about to rock your world and things might get a little out of control."

Nichole's breath hardens as she opens her mouth slightly letting out her breath. She's so responsive and I haven't even touched her yet. I fucking love it.

"Is there anything you don't like?"

Nichole bites her lower lip again, shaking her head *no*. Again, speechless. I wonder where my voicetress girl from last night went. Tonight she's all quiet, submissive and I'm loving every second.

Don't get me wrong, last night was great, but this new, submissive, almost shy girl is rocking my world just the same.

I take a deep breath in, speaking in a low voice, "I'm going to fuck you into oblivion." I swoop her up, throwing her against the wall, pressing my hard body against hers. She wraps her legs around my waist as I press my lips firmly to her, forcing her mouth open as my tongue invades her mouth, exploring, demanding, pulsating through her body.

Our kiss is more passionate than I planned and my heart starts to race as I unzip my pants, pushing her panties to the side and force myself inside her, slamming her against the wall.

My thrusts are intense as I push her up and down, pounding into her as hard as I can.

Changing positions, I move to toss her on the bed, removing my pants completely before leaning down to remove her panties. I lick her clit as I stick two fingers inside her.

"Fuck, you are so wet."

I tilt my head down in disbelief from how bad I want to take her in every position possible.

Grabbing a condom, I slip it on and slide inside her again as I stand with her legs up on my shoulders.

Slow at first, I start a rhythmic motion, bringing her higher and higher.

I start to pound hard inside her, then pause, pulling out as slowly as I can before starting my movement all over.

I feel like I could explode at any minute, but when I stop, my face relaxes and a smile spreads over my face before I start all over again.

I'm lost to everything I feel rushing through my body, but I almost blow my load when I feel her body tighten around me, bringing her to the most intense orgasm, making her toes curl, her knees buckle and head fall back in ecstasy.

I'm surprised to feel her cum so fast, especially when I wasn't doing anything special to bring her to that point, so I bend down, whispering in her ear, "Fuck baby… and we've just started. That's one…"

I pull back, smiling a cocky smile before flipping her over to her stomach. I love how I can do with her as I please.

I caress her ass before leaning down to lick between her legs. "Mmm, you taste so good."

I lie on top of her, keeping her legs closed and thrust inside of her again, moving ever so slowly to rebuild her pleasure.

She lies there, completely relaxed, and I know she's still reeling from her orgasm as I continue my pace.

I pound into her, grabbing her ass and spanking it hard. Damn, it barely moves it's so tight. Running my fingers up her back, I push her head down on the mattress more, tilting her ass for the perfect view.

Suddenly her legs clinch tighter and tighter around me so I reach around, caressing her breast before pulling on her nipple. I must have hit just the right spot because she responds instantly and erupts around me again.

I can't help my grin against her back as I whisper, "That's two."

She's too weak to even smile. Her head is in a daze at the intense orgasms so close together and I feel like a sex God right now.

I flip her again so she's lying on her back. "Just wait till you feel this."

I thrust inside her as I lie on top of her, missionary style. She squirms under me, trying to flip me over but the two orgasms have taken their toll and she's too weak.

I'm surprised she's not into this position. Women seem to always want it and normally I stay far away because it feels so "coupley" and I only like to fuck, with no emotion so I avoid it at all cost but for some reason it feels right tonight.

She tries to flip me over again but I say firmly, "No you don't. I'm in control here."

I lean down, kissing her lips as I slowly pull in and out of her. She lifts her legs up to wrap around my waist, finally giving in and throwing her head back.

I grab her wrists, pulling them back behind her head, holding onto them, making me in complete control as I bring her to her third orgasm of the night.

Clenching my teeth, I forcefully say, "That's three," as I cum, moaning loudly as I fall down on her, wrapping my arms under her back and holding her tightly. We lay like that for a few moments while we catch our breath.

Nichole gets up, walking to the bathroom and after I discard of the condom, I curl up under her covers with my arm resting behind my back, turning the TV back on to *Sports Center*.

When she walks back she lets out a sharp laugh, "Well, make yourself right at home."

"I think I will. I won the challenge didn't I?" I say as cocky as I can.

Nichole laughs, "Ok, I'll give you that. That was hot. But come on, time to go."

I stick my lower lip out, tilting my head to one side, pouting, "Are you kicking me out?"

"I told you, I don't do sleepovers."

"Well, I'm all about breaking the rules with you and if you don't do sleepovers then you don't know what it is to have morning-after sex," I raise my eyebrows to her. I can't believe I want to stay either but I really just want to fall asleep right here. I'm on such a high right now and I want it to last.

"What are you talking about?"

"Damn, you're in for a treat, especially after that pounding I just gave you."

"Oh, really?"

I grab her arm, pulling her down to the bed, whispering as sexy as I can. "You're going to sleep next to me all night, dreaming of the time we just had, and when you wake up and see me next to you, you'll want more." I kiss her neck before going on. "And when I stick it in, you will be sore from our time tonight, but so horny because of the memories and you will love every minute of it."

Nichole tilts her head to the side, allowing me to further my kiss on her neck, "Mmm, is that a promise?"

I stop to look at her, "You know it is. Now get under the covers. You'll need your rest."

She hops up first and grabs my old blue shirt I gave her last night and slips it on.

"You like my shirt?"

Nichole grabs it, smiling, "Maybe."

"Good. I like seeing it on you. What do you have planned tomorrow?"

"My new campaign comes out. I'm going to go grab a copy of *Cosmopolitan* to see it."

"Campaign?"

"Yeah, I'm a model and I just did a Calvin Klein shoot. It's in the new issue that comes out tomorrow."

"Shut the fuck up. I'm fucking a model?"

"Um no. You just fucked a model. We aren't fucking."

I grab her, pulling her in close, "Oh, we are fucking. I've made you cum multiple times now. I'd say that's fucking," I respond, kissing her neck.

"That doesn't mean it's going to keep happening."

I laugh, "Yes it does. Don't fight it. You like this dick. Admit it. We are fucking. And we're going to keep fucking."

Nichole rolls her eyes at me but doesn't answer.

I look at her sternly, "And I only fuck one person at a time, so that better be mutual."

Nichole's mouth forms a small smile that she can't hide.

"See, you can't fight it. You love this dick," I smack her ass. "Now get in bed."

I reach to turn off the TV when I see my phone vibrating on the floor. Hitting ignore to the call it shows me I have four missed calls and seven text messages, all from Beth.

God. Fucking. Dammit.

I don't read them or listen to the messages. Just power the phone off so she doesn't keep us up all night. Lord knows I don't want Nichole to find out. Why can't she just leave me alone once and for all?

I crawl back under the covers and click the TV off, forgetting about my phone. "Don't forget to dream about me," I taunt.

Nichole rolls her eyes before lying on her side, away from me but I don't care. I won the battle. I'm staying the night and have all night to dream about how I'm going to rock her world again tomorrow.

When morning arrives I curl up next to her, pushing my hard cock against her.

"Well, good morning Paul," she smiles.

"Hmm, good morning. Are you horny for me?"

She tries to play it off like she isn't but when I wrap my arm around her to rub on the outside of her panties I can feel how wet she already is. "Oh yeah, what did I tell you? You dreamt about me didn't you?"

Nichole laughs, "A lady never tells."

"Well good thing you're not a lady."

I start to pull off her lace panties, kissing the back of her neck before slipping on a condom.

As we lay on our sides, with her legs held tightly together, I thrust inside her making her moan in absolute delight.

I keep up my delicious torture of her body, taking her higher and higher. She has no chance of being able to stay quiet and screams out in pleasure.

Allison

We walk into my apartment to grab my smaller camera for our trip back to Vacaville for Mason's birthday party. Once we get to our floor level both of us look to each other laughing.

"Holy shit," Charlie yells out.

"Oh my God. What? Who? Um, shit," I laugh.

"Get it girl!" Charlie yells out.

I hit his stomach "Shhhh... They don't know we're here. Wait, God, I hope she has someone in there with her."

Charlie laughs, "Um yes, I would say she does."

"No, I mean, she's never, I mean never, had a guy stay the night."

Charlie lifts his eyebrows. "Well, she did last night. Goddamn. Oh shit, did you ever hear if anything happened with Paul the other night?"

I shake my head. "No, I haven't talked to her."

We can hear them both cum, one after the other and then silence falls from her room. We sit stunned, trying hard not to laugh.

Not long after, Paul opens the door, surprised to see us standing there.

Charlie starts laughing, turning around since Paul is still naked. "Yeah! That's my boy," he yells out.

"Oh, shit," Paul covers himself, running into the bathroom, "Sorry Allison. What's up, bro?" he nods to Charlie with his cocky smile.

I look at Charlie with my eyes open wide and we both laugh.

Nichole walks out of her room wearing a guys blue shirt that I've never seen before. She stops in her tracks when she see's Charlie standing in the kitchen and turns bright red.

Charlie smiles big before teasing her, "I see you've had a good morning."

Nichole taunts, "With your line of work, that should be a normal event."

Charlie's mouth forms a straight line and my stomach turns instantly.

"Come on, I quit. Please don't bring that up," he begs.

Nichole shrugs her shoulders, "Sorry..." before walking back into her room.

Paul steps out of the bathroom with a pink towel wrapped around his waist. "What's up, bro?" he walks to Charlie with his hand out.

"I'd ask you the same thing but I think the entire building can answer that for you," Charlie laughs.

"Hey, what can I say? I'm that good."

"Oh God, I'm out of here. No need to make that ego any bigger," I say as I follow Nichole into her bedroom.

"Holy shit girl. So I take it things went well the other night after you left?"

Nichole looks at me, trying to act nonchalantly, "Yeah, I guess so."

I slap her arm, "Shut up. You like him."

"God, Allison. He's just a good fuck. As you can tell," she smirks.

"Don't lie. Did he really stay the night? And look, where did this t-shirt come from?"

Nichole looks down, "It's his. He let me wear it home yesterday morning. It's comfy, that's all."

"Wait, you stayed at his place the other night?"

"Ugh, yes. What's the big deal?"

I laugh as I look away, teasing Nichole, "Oh, nothing…"

"Stop. I'm not you. I don't date. You know this."

"Yeah, you also don't let guys sleep over or stay at their house," I get up, putting my hands up in defense. "But hey, I believe you. It's nothing," I laugh. "Love you. We're heading to Vacaville for his friend's son's birthday party. See you later. Enjoy your comfy shirt."

I walk out of Nichole's room to see Charlie and Paul talking in the kitchen. I look at Paul, laughing at the pink towel wrapped around him, "Ok lover boy. Go put some clothes on."

Paul smirks, raising his eyebrows, "See you guys later."

I turn to Charlie, whispering, "He not only stayed the night here, she stayed at his place the other night."

"So?" Charlie responds, confused.

"No, this is a big deal. She never stays with anyone."

"Well, good. He's a good guy," he leans in, giving me a small kiss, "Come on, let's go."

Nine

Allison

We drive to Vacaville for Mason's birthday party at a local park. As we walk up to the party, Mason and Leighton come running up to Charlie, tackling him like they always do.

"Hey Guys," Charlie yells out as they jump on him. "Happy birthday, Mason. Look at what I got you?"

He hands Mason a gift bag that he tears open instantly, grabbing the football that Charlie got him. "Cool! Thanks Uncle Charlie. Come on, let's play," Mason says tugging on his arm.

Charlie looks at me, smiling. I just laugh and continue my walk up to where Jason, Jen and their families are sitting.

"Allison," Jen holds her arms open for a hug as I approach. We embrace as Jen says, "I'm so glad you're here. Let me introduce you to everyone. These are my parents, Tim and Sue, my best friend, Alicia, and over here are Jason's parents, Steve and Carol. This is Charlie's girlfriend, Allison."

"Oh, Allison. It is so nice to meet you," Carol jumps up, wrapping her arms around me.

"It's nice to meet you, too."

"Mom, jeez, don't be so obvious," Jason yells out.

Carol laughs, "Sorry. It's just that Charlie has always been like a son to us. We are so happy to hear he has found someone."

Steve reaches out his hand, "Allison, it's a pleasure to meet you finally."

I sit down on the picnic table with everyone and watch Charlie play catch with Mason. The look on his face melts my heart. He is so at ease with Mason and I can tell he loves every minute of playing catch.

He really does want to be a dad. Ugh, I just wish it wasn't like this. I wish it was with me... Our baby... Later on, down the road...

"Allison?" Jen says, taking me out of my daydream. "Would you like a slice of Pizza?"

"Sorry, yes, please," I grab the plate while Carol sits down next to me to eat.

"So, Allison, how did you and Charlie meet?" Carol asks.

I light up at the chance to tell our story. "Funny story really. We saw each other at a concert for our favorite band, Unwritten Law, in the City, but it wasn't till he saw me sitting at Starbucks the next day that he came up to say hello."

"Oh, I love it," Carol claps her hands together, "Just like you guys were meant to be."

I smile, "I like to think so."

"So what do you do for a living?"

"I actually just finished photography school. We just got back from Paris where I had an internship and I got to shoot some of Paris' Fashion Week."

"That's wonderful. I don't know what that is but it sounds fabulous." Carol laughs. "I'm not up on the whole fashion world."

Jason jumps in, "Yeah, if it doesn't have anything to do with a good book or her church, Mom doesn't know it exists."

"Don't lie, I know some things. I just got my first Smartphone didn't I?"

Jason laughs even harder, "See what I mean? She just got one. Mason had to show her how to work it, too. It's ok Mom, I still love you."

"I love you, too, honey," Carol pats his hand.

Charlie is smiling the entire way home. He loves playing with those boys and they really bring out a special side of him. My heart starts to break even more just watching how happy he is.

I knew he couldn't stop this pregnancy. Really, I should love him more for that. But man, why does it hurt so bad? I want it to be our baby. Not his and a crazy woman who paid him for sex. Ugh, at least she won't be part of the picture. My God, that would just be the cherry on top. There is no way I could deal with that. I drop my head back as the thought makes my stomach turn.

Charlie turns down the radio, "What's wrong, baby?"

I perk up instantly, trying to pretend, "Oh, nothing. Just tired. Still on Paris time, you know."

Charlie reaches out his hand, gripping mine, "You sure?"

I smile, trying to change the subject, "Yeah. So how long have Jason and Jen been married?"

"Gosh, this is Mason's seventh birthday so a little more than eight years, I guess. Wow, that went by fast." He looks at me with what looks like hope in his eyes. "Maybe we will be there one day?"

My stomach is still turning and hearing him say that makes it turn a little more. I smile back as I can't get any words out in fear of throwing up.

I do want to marry you, Charlie. I wanted to spend to the rest of my life with you but now, now I just don't know.

I look out the window as a small tear falls down my face.

My phone beeps with a text message from Nichole:

> Hey, you two heading back yet? Paul and I wanted to go out tonight, you guys want to come too?

I look at Charlie, "Paul and Nichole want us to go out tonight. You up for it?"

"Sure, sounds like fun. What did they have in mind?"

I text back:

> Sure! Where do you want to go?

> Thinking Ruby Skye. I want to dance with his sexy ass.

I roll my eyes at both my sister's reply and her choice of where to go. I never told her what happened last time we were there.

I look at Charlie, "They want to go to Ruby Skye…"

Charlie laughs, "You promise you won't dance with another guy?"

I snap back, instantly pissed off by his comment, "You promise one of your clients won't kidnap and threaten to kill me again?"

Charlie glares back at me. I know he's shocked I would say something like that but I don't care. He crossed a line and needs to know.

"Allison…" he pulls off at the next exit, coming to a stop as soon as he can. He drops his head to his steering wheel not saying a word.

I sit back in my seat, crossing my arms in frustration.

"Allison, I thought we were over this. I can't even begin to tell you how sorry I am that happened to you." He looks at me with his eyes sagging he's so ashamed.

I can't stand to see him look like this and my frustration eases slightly. "I'm sorry, Charlie. That was a low blow. It's just… I'm sorry."

I can't bring myself to say what I'm thinking or feeling. My thoughts of Jacquelyn and the baby brought back feelings I've tried to compress and it was just bad timing.

That's all that was, just bad timing.

Charlie leans over to hug me tightly, "I know you'll never forget what happened but please know that I'll do everything in my power to make you as happy as you can possibly be."

"I know," I hug him back and I'm not lying. I know he is sorry and that he loves me. I just don't know if I can forget.

He starts to turn the car around and get back on the freeway. "Maybe we should suggest somewhere else to go."

"No, we can't let what happen dictate our lives. Besides, remember the last time we went dancing?" I lift my eyebrows to him, remembering our time in Paris at the VIP Room.

Charlie's eyes light up as he looks at me, "Do I ever…"

I smile back, glad that happy memories of us together have filled the air around us. "Ok then."

I text back to Nichole:

Sounds good. Meet at Charlie's place?

Come up to Paul's. You have to check this place out!

"She said to meet up at Paul's place. She wants me to check it out."

"Oh shit, I didn't even think about that. You said that Nichole stayed at his place, right?"

"Yeah…?"

He looks at me, shaking his head up and down, "Damn. Ok, maybe you were right about them making a connection. You said that Nichole never has guys stay the night, right?"

"Yeah."

"Well, Paul has a strict no girl in his apartment rule."

"What? That's weird."

"Wait till you see his place."

"Ok, why? I don't get it."

"He's an architect. He actually designed the building I live in."

"Shut up. Paul, the guy with all the tattoos, is a high-end architect?"

Charlie laughs, "Yup. Hard to believe, huh?"

"Um, yes. I would have never imagined that. Wait, so why the no girl rule?"

"He has the top floor penthouse in my building. Since he was the architect, he built it to be exactly what he wanted and man, it is bad ass."

"So, I don't get it. Why wouldn't he want to show it off to girls?"

"He's pretty adamant about girls not wanting him just cause he has money, so he acts just like a normal dude and doesn't show them."

"That's weird, why have this huge place if you don't want to show it off?"

He stops to think, "Not sure. I've never really thought about it I guess. Just thought it made sense. He always says, 'I don't want no gold digging whore,'" Charlie laughs.

I sit back in my seat, "Hmmm, maybe we made a connection for them after all."

We walk into the elevator, and Charlie presses the 49th floor plus a four-digit code.

I look at Charlie, "Wow, you weren't kidding."

"No, I wasn't," he laughs.

Nichole comes walking out of Paul's bedroom when she hears us arrive. "Hey guys. You ready to go dance your ass off?"

"Yeah. Man, you weren't kidding about this place," Allison says in shock.

Nichole smiles, still trying to act like it's not *that* big of a deal. "Yeah, it's cool."

Paul walks up, smacking her ass, "Cool my ass. My place is the shit! Here, I'll show you around."

He walks me through the 3,200 square feet of his apartment, with every detail thought out and executed to the highest quality. There are two other bedrooms, two balconies and a study off the master bedroom.

Once back in the living room where Charlie and Nichole are sitting, I look at Paul, "Wow Paul, this place is amazing. But why? Why have something so big if only you live here?"

Paul thinks for a second, "I don't know. For something more one day I guess."

He looks at Nichole and they catch eyes, which surprises the hell out of me. Who knows what's going on in Nichole's head from that comment.

Nichole jumps up, and my intuition was right. She's totally freaked out by what he just said. "Ok. Let's get out of here," she says walking away from Paul.

We walk up to Ruby Skye to see the same bouncer working the front door from the last time they were there. As Charlie approaches the bouncer holds up his hands trying to block his face, teasing Charlie, "Oh no, Mike Tyson's back."

"Awe man," he looks at me and I just glare back. "Sorry about that," he says to the bouncer as they grip hands.

"Hey, it's all good. She's hot. I'd knock a guy out for her, too," he laughs. "Go on in."

"Thanks bro. Ladies, after you."

Charlie grabs us all a round of drinks as we stand around a tall table, taking in the scene around us. Nichole downs her drink, anxious to start the night off right, then heads out to the dance floor alone while we sit back watching.

"So, no girl in your apartment rule flew out the window pretty fast, huh?" Charlie asks Paul.

"Fuck dude, don't remind me. She's sexy as hell though."

"Yeah, I guess, if you like that model type," Charlie smirks, winking at me.

"Fuck yeah I do!" Paul yells obnoxiously. "I'd drink her bath water," he jokes.

Charlie chokes on his beer, laughing, "Only you, Paul."

I'm grossed out by his comment so I drink the last drop of my drink and head out to join Nichole.

Paul downs his beer and follows us out to the dance floor with Charlie right behind him. Paul walks up behind Nichole while Charlie walks up in front of me. Both wrapping their arms around us like they're claiming our bodies, dancing seductively.

The song changes as Rihanna's *We Found Love* begins to play.

Charlie and I intertwine as we move with the beat, kissing with our hands lacing around each other's.

I look over at Paul who's still behind Nichole with his arms wrapped around her hips and her arms wrapped behind his head. He kisses her neck as they seductively move slower than the dance beat playing around them. Both of them moving slower and slower until they're swaying, holding each other close, rubbing against each other.

They look completely lost in the moment and I'm shocked. This is so not like Nichole. They stop moving, standing still, holding on to one another tightly. Paul starts to rub his hands up her body and around her breasts. Both of them have the most intense look on their faces.

The end of the song talks about finding love in a hopeless place and I watch as Paul turns Nichole around, kissing her deeply, holding her up against him. I stop dancing, hitting Charlie's chest, motioning to check them out.

The next song begins as he lets go, pulling back to look at her.

Nichole backs up slowly, saying something to him and starts to walk off the dance floor toward the bar, holding his hand. I grab Charlie to follow them.

"Shall we order another round?" I yell out, looking at Nichole who is pale white and trying to not look at Paul. I turn to Charlie, "Hey, Nichole and I are going to the ladies room, will you get us another round?"

"Sure thing."

Both guys are clueless as I grab Nichole's arm, pulling her to the bathroom. Once the door is shut I turn to her, "Wow, what's going on? I've never seen you look so, so, I'm not sure. What happened out there?"

Nichole shakes her head and I'm sure she realizes now why we're in the bathroom. "I don't know what you're talking about." She turns to the mirror to check her make-up.

"Don't lie. Something happened. I saw it and can read it all over your face."

"Oh, stop. Nothing happened. I was probably just flush from dancing."

"Yeah, dancing with Paul. You are really falling for this guy, aren't you?"

She gives me a give-me-a-break look, "Really? I've known him for all of what, three days."

"Yeah, and you've seen him everyday. What did you do today by the way, Nichole?"

"We just hung out," she shrugs her shoulders. "Got the new magazine I'm in, walked around downtown, had lunch. No big deal."

"No big deal...? Ha! Ok, fine, say what you want. But I saw it. I saw something on your face that you can't deny."

Nichole shoots me a grim look, "I'm not you remember. I don't date." She storms out of the bathroom; mad that I noticed what she was feeling.

Nichole proceeds to get pretty drunk. I know she's trying to hide her feelings for Paul but dancing as provocatively as she can with him isn't pleading her case with me.

The night ends and we all pour out of the club, heading back to Charlie and Paul's building. Nichole doesn't notice where we are heading until we're in front of their building. "Whoa, wait. I need to go home," she proclaims in her very drunk state.

Paul grabs her, "No, you're staying here tonight."

"What part of I-don't-do-sleep-overs are you not understanding?" she asks as she sways back and forth, trying to stand up straight.

"Well, get over it. Now you do." He picks her up, throwing her over his shoulder as they walk into the lobby.

Charlie and I laugh as the elevator doors open. Nichole tries to fight back but is laughing uncontrollably. "Do you have your phone in your ass?" Nichole laughs obviously meaning his pocket. "I can hear your ass ringing from down here."

Paul reaches in his back pocket with his free hand and silences it without looking to see who is calling.

Once in the elevator, Paul puts her down, smacking her ass, "Good girl."

"Fine, but I'm sleeping in one of the other bedrooms," she folds her arms across her chest.

"Deal. That is, after we fuck…" he pulls her into his arms.

"Well yeah, that was a given," she teases back.

"This could be fun. We can break in every room in my house with this attitude."

Charlie and I look at each other, "Damn, they're making us look bad over here, babe," I hit Charlie's chest as his floor dings its arrival.

He swoops in, picking me up, throwing me over his shoulder, "Not for long they aren't. Later you two."

I laugh as I wave goodbye to my sister from upside down.

Charlie

Allison and I are eating lunch together, enjoying a quiet day alone when my phone rings. "Hello, Diane."

"Charlie, did you not call the Detective?"

"No, I haven't. Why?"

"Well, he just called me and is wanting to speak to you."

"Why?"

"Because you are the father of this baby. He knows that. Just act like nothing is wrong. It looks worse that you are avoiding him."

"Fine. I'll call him right now."

"No, wait thirty minutes. I told him I was not home and I did not have your number. It would look obvious if you called him right away."

"Fine, Diane. Goodbye," I hang up the phone and look at Allison who is sitting next to me as we eat lunch together.

"What did she want?" Allison says disgusted.

"Come on Allison, you will have to forgive her at some point."

Allison rolls her eyes at me.

"I guess the detective in Jacquelyn's case wants to talk to me."

Allison jumps up, "Why? How do they even know who you are?"

I look down, ashamed, "Because she's pregnant and I'm the father, remember?"

Allison looks down and I lean in to hug her but this time she doesn't hug back. "Allison, please don't be upset."

Her voice is stern when she responds, "Charlie, I told you. I need time."

I put my head down, backing away from her, moving my fork around my plate, not sure if I can take another bite.

We sit in an awkward silence as we clean up our lunch before I walk into the other room to call the Detective.

"Detective O'Brien," he answers.

"Hi, this is Charlie Ashley. I hear you wanted to talk to me about Jacquelyn Sanders."

"Oh, yes, Charlie Ashley. Can you come into the station so we can discuss a few things?"

"Um, can't you ask me what you need over the phone?"

"I'd rather you come in. When can you come down?"

"Ok, I can head there right now if that works for you."

"Perfect, I'll be here."

I walk back into the room where Allison is. "I need to go to the police station. Would you like to come?"

"Why would I want to come to the police station? I told you, I don't want anything to do with all of this."

I stop, not sure what to say. "Even the baby?" I finally whisper.

"Time, Charlie. I said to give me time," she looks down. "Look, I'll go home. You go to the station. Just call me when you get back."

"No, Allison, this is your home," I grab her to try to bring our loving mood back.

"Charlie," she looks away. "I told you… time…"

"Ok, but please stay. I won't be long."

"It's ok. I actually need to go talk to Alex anyway. I'll head down there and meet you back here later, ok?"

I lean in to kiss her, "Ok."

I walk into the police station and am escorted back to Detective O'Brien's office.

"Detective O'Brien? Hi, I'm Charlie Ashley." I reach out to shake the Detective's hand.

"Hi. Thank you for coming down. Please, sit," he motions to me. "So, how did you know Jacquelyn Sanders?"

I've practiced what I should say but now that I'm here, nerves start to take over. "Um, we dated a few times."

"So, how long have you known her?"

"Not long."

"And now she's pregnant with your baby? How do you feel about that?"

"I'm not sure if that matters in what you're trying to accomplish here?" I snap back.

Detective O'Brien shakes his head, "Ok. So, where were you when she was shot?"

I shake my head, "That was a month ago, I don't remember exactly what I was doing. I don't even know what time of day she was shot."

"Really, well, weren't you dating her?"

"No, we ended a few days before she was shot."

"Oh, really…?"

"Hey, it was no big deal. We only dated a few times. Never anything serious. She wanted more and I didn't so we ended it. No big deal."

"Yeah, you said that already. When did you find out she was shot?"

"Not until I was already in Paris."

"So, a woman you dated, gets shot in her entryway and no one tells you?"

"No, sorry. We don't have mutual friends and I live in the City so it's not like I read a San Rafael paper or anything."

"That reminds me. You do have a mutual friend, Diane Hayes. She's the one that called you in Paris, right?"

"Yes, she did."

"She's the one that found Jacquelyn."

"Um, ok…"

"And you two obviously know each other if she knew how to get a hold of you in Paris, so why didn't she think you should know she was shot to begin with?"

"I don't know? You'll have to ask her. It's not like I talk to her often. I told you. Jacquelyn and I only dated a few times. It was never anything big. That's probably why she didn't tell me."

"So, how do you know Diane then?"

"We're friends from the gym we attend in the City, Life Fitness. She introduced me to Jacquelyn there."

"So, how did she know how to get a hold of you in Paris?"

"She knew I was there for a modeling gig. That's why it took her so long to get a hold of me though, she had to contact the agency and get a hold of me that way."

"Is that what you do for a living, modeling?"

"Well, um, trying to be. Really I'm a customer service rep for Livingston, Inc."

I had this entire thing figured out in my head but I never thought the questioning would go to this. I'm thankful I'm able to think quickly but not sure if I'm digging myself a bigger hole. I just need to make sure Allison is not brought up.

"What modeling agency do you work for?"

"Not one in particular. I went knowing there would be work. That's why it took her so long to find me. She had to ask around for someone who knew me."

Detective O'Brien shakes his head and I have no clue if he is buying all of this.

After taking some notes he looks up at me, "Ok, I think that will do for now. I have your number so I'll be in touch."

I shake his hand and leave the police station with a big sigh of relief, feeling the meeting went well.

Allison

My hands start to tremble as I walk up to the building Alex's studio is in. The memory of Jacquelyn forcing me into the car races through my mind as my stomach ties in knots and I fight the urge to throw up, or faint, or maybe both.

My face flushes and my palms sweat as I get the courage to walk up to the entrance. Trying to push the thought out of my head, I run into the building.

As I enter the studio Alex is standing in the reception area talking to the receptionist. I watch him light up as I walk in. "Allison! How are you?"

"I'm good," I say though not very convincingly.

He walks up to me, "Hey, are you ok?"

I shake my head up and down saying, "I'm fine," as tears fill my eyes.

"No you're not. Here come back to my office."

"No, no, it's ok," I stutter, gaining my composure. "I know you wanted me to check in with you so, here I am," I try to smile and sound happy.

Alex smiles, "Ok, yes, come on back."

We walk back to his office and I sit down, looking at the proofs sitting on his desk. "Wow, these look great."

"Yes, they do. I present them to the client later today so let's hope they will think so, too. So, I wanted to talk to you about what your plans were now that you're graduated."

"Well…" I start to answer and Alex interrupts me before I can say anything.

"Sorry, before you say anything, I want to offer you a position here, at my studio as my first assistant."

I jump up, "Are you serious? That's amazing. Thank you so much," I wrap my arms around him, hugging him tightly.

Alex laughs, hugging me back lightly, "So, I take it you accept?"

"Oh, sorry," I step back embarrassed. I can't believe I just hugged him like that. "Yes, I accept. Thank you so much for this opportunity."

"Great. We have a photo shoot scheduled for tomorrow. Can you come in around ten?"

"Of course. Thank you again. I'll see you tomorrow."

When I arrive back at Charlie's place he is already home and I run in, yelling, "Charlie, are you home?"

"Yeah, what's up, baby?" he comes out of the bedroom to greet me.

"Alex just offered me a job as his first assistant!" I jump up and down excitedly, running toward him.

Charlie runs up, grabbing me, swinging me around, saying, "Oh, Allison. That's wonderful. I'm so proud of you." Then he kisses me.

His kiss melts my insides, reminding me how much I love him and pushing the insecurities from before when I was reminded of the baby out of my mind.

Electricity runs through my body as he pulls back to look in my eyes. I know he feels it, too. He lightly kisses me again then smiles.

Wrapping his hand in my hair, he leans in, kissing me softly, slowly picking me up, he walks me into the bedroom whispering, "I'm the luckiest man in the world to have found you."

"Charlie," I whisper back, leaning up to kiss him again.

"I mean it Allison. My world didn't make sense until I met you. You have saved me in more ways than I could ever explain."

He doesn't wait for my reply as he lays me down, kissing me softly. I'm filled with intense emotions that I can't deny. His touch alone makes every thought in my mind disappear. No matter what is going through my head on a daily basis about Jacquelyn and the baby, all Charlie needs to do is kiss me, touch me, and I know I'm his forever.

I start to run my fingers through his hair, pulling him in closer, trying to show him how much I want him.

He pulls my shirt up then removes his own. The feeling of our skin touching makes us both moan as he kisses down my neck to my chest with his hands behind me, gripping me tightly like he can't hold me close enough.

After removing my pants, then his, he lays down, thrusting inside me. He kisses my lips softly, moving his body in and out.

Every touch, every motion lights me on fire. I can't get enough and I match him thrust for thrust, curving my hips up, trying to get him inside me as far as he can go.

He flips me around so I'm on top and I grab the back of the bed while he leans up to suck on my nipple.

Holy shit!

I can't take it anymore and I start to grind myself against him. Riding him harder than I ever have before. Holding the headboard tightly before I lose it completely.

I start to beg. No, scream for my release to reach pure heaven. He gives me exactly what I'm looking for while he grunts his own release.

Afterward I lie on his chest, sighing my relaxation, asking, "Do men get the same feeling after sex that women do?"

Charlie laughs, "Um, not sure. What do you mean?"

"It's this euphoria that engulfs your entire body with a sense of complete happiness and relaxation. I just want to lay here and enjoy it forever."

"Really...?"

"It's amazing. I can only imagine it's the best feeling on earth. Better than any drug."

"Wow. And it's free. Well, for you at least," he smirks.

I hit his chest shocked he just said that.

"What? Too soon?" he says laughing.

I can't help but laugh at his joke though I'm not happy about it, "Yes, too soon."

PAUL

I'm with a group of older men dressed in suits standing around a long black table as I explain the drawings on the blueprints in front of us. The thin paper keeps rolling back into the roll so I set my phone on the corner of the blueprints to keep them in place while my hand holds the other side.

"Now gentlemen, as you can see, when we put the elevator over here, it opens up this wing for easier access to have two gym areas, which will be a huge selling point for the penthouse apartments. This way they will have their own private gym."

My phone is on vibrate and it shakes showing a call coming in. My client looks down and scours his eyebrows, handing me the phone, obviously irritated by it. "I take it this is a call you want to take?"

I grab it and see the Calvin Klein ad of Nichole with "I'm Fucking a Model" written as the name. I gasp since I had no idea Nichole programmed my phone with her number, let alone like that.

"I must apologize. That is extremely inappropriate. She must have been playing with my phone. I really had no idea it was programmed like that." I silence the phone and stick it in my pocket, trying to move on with my client like nothing happened.

Once I'm back in my office, I pick up the phone and smirk as I see the missed call saying "I'm Fucking a Model." Smiling, I redial her number. This chick just keeps getting better and better.

"Well, hello there," Nichole answers.

"So, I did get your number after all."

"Yeah, I liked making you think I wouldn't give it to you though."

"I love the reminder of who I'm fucking but my client who handed it to me didn't think it was as cute."

Nichole laughs out loud, "Shit, sorry. What did they say?"

"Nothing, thankfully. They didn't look too pleased though. You're lucky I'm digging your sexy ass," I laugh.

"Well… can I make it up to you tonight? Say, my house at ten?"

"No, I'll pick you up at seven to take you to dinner." Wow, that came out of nowhere. I never take a girl to dinner but it just felt right and I didn't even think about it before I said it. Now that I have though, I'm almost excited about where to take her.

"I told you, that's not necessary."

"Well, I think you need to make something up to me so I say it is necessary."

"Fine. You can take me to In-n-Out."

"Ha! Just for that I'm going to take you to the most romantic restaurant I can find."

"No, really. Just come over at ten. Maybe I'll let you stay the night again to make it up to you."

I smirk, "I'll be there at seven. Be ready," then hang up before she can dispute me anymore.

A few minutes later my text message dings with a link to a YouTube video from Nichole. The video starts off kind of crazy showing naked kissing girls, S&M play and animals. I'm kind of shocked a girl would send me something like this, even from someone like Nichole. That is until I hear the words to *Casual Sex* by My Darkest Days talking about a couple not dating, just having hardcore casual sex.

I text back:

OH IT'S ON NOW… BE READY AT 7

I text Charlie, hoping Allison can help me out as more ideas for tonight pop into my head.

CAN YOU ASK ALLISON WHAT SIZE NICHOLE IS FOR A DRESS?

She says 4 but wants to know why?

SHE'LL SEE. THANKS BRO.

At seven exactly I ring Nichole's doorbell. She answers and I get the exact reaction I was waiting for. Shock, surprise and finally, lust written all over her face and I fucking love it.

I'm wearing black suit pants, a tie and a vest with a dress shirt underneath, smiling slightly while holding a Versace bag out to her.

"Shut up," Nichole says. "What is this? I said you could take me to In-n-out."

"And I said I would take you to the most romantic place I know. I'm keeping my word. Here, go put this on."

Nichole tries to hide her smile but I see it as she asks defiantly, "How do you know it will fit?"

"I have my ways. Now, go get dressed," I say in a low whispering voice.

Turning around, she walks up the stairs as I walk through the door and shut it behind me.

"Are you going to come in and watch me change?" she offers.

"No, I want to see you come out, displaying for me the beauty I see in you, even with all of your clothes on." Damn, did I really just say that? I shake my head, realizing even more that this chick is really starting to get to me.

While I'm in the kitchen waiting my phone goes off three times. *Fuck, Beth, not now. Leave me the hell alone!*

She opens the door just as I'm powering down my phone and slipping it in my back pocket. We lock eyes and my face lights up as she walks toward me. She turns around to give me the entire view of the white, floor length gown with a plunging neckline all the way to her stomach leaving her cleavage completely open. Rhinestones moving all the way up from her hips to her breast in horizontal rows line the sides, showing her bare skin underneath.

Her hair was originally down and I'm so glad she decided to pull it up, leaving a few strands around, exposing the back of her neck and looking sexy as hell.

My chest tightens and I grab it, whispering, "Nichole…"

"You like?"

"Wow, the hanger did it no justice. You look amazing."

"Well, so do you. Now where are you taking me?"

"It's a surprise. After you…"

She gives me a small kiss on the lips, "Thank you for the dress."

"You're more than welcome. Seeing you in it is the best present I've ever received."

We walk down the staircase and Nichole turns to me, "Wait, there is no way I can get on the back of a motorcycle in this dress."

"I know, that's why I got us this…" I point to a stretch limo sitting a few doors up from her house with a chauffeur holding the door open, waiting for us to get in.

"You have got to be kidding me. Paul, you've lost your mind."

I grab her hand. "This way I can fuck you through the streets of San Francisco. The way you look in that dress is making it hard to contain myself. But first, dinner."

I'm not sure why I just said that, I have no intention of having sex with her in the limo. Crazy, I know, but I never even thought about it when I reserved the car. All I could think about was putting a smile on her face and being here, in this moment, I'm realizing that sex never even came to my mind and I'm shocked that it didn't. This is the first time I've done something for a girl that didn't revolve around getting in her panties. The thought should freak me out but surprisingly it's not.

Nichole walks to the limo and sits down, smiling as I sit beside her, grabbing her hand. "I thought the dress was present enough for me but I was wrong. That smile is the best thing I've ever seen." I lean in and kiss her softly as the limo drives away.

We drive to the Mission District to a place called Lazy Bear. As she steps out of the car Nichole looks at me, "Wait, how did you pull this off? You have to buy tickets to this place that are nearly impossible to get."

I lean down to whisper, "I'm the architect that designed it. I know the owner and did it more as a favor so I called in a favor in return." I wink at her as I escort her inside.

We enter the restaurant to see two long tables with an open kitchen at the end of the long room. Wanting it to feel more like a dinner party, rather than a normal restaurant, the Lazy Bear only offers communal seating and two serving times for its guests so everyone shares their dining experience.

I thought it would be perfect, taking away any insecurities Nichole may have felt at a romantic restaurant with just the two of us seated together.

A hostess shows us to the end of the table, closest to the kitchen area. The chef sees me and instantly walks over to us. "Paul!" He reaches out his hand to shake mine. "You finally made it in. We're so glad you decided to join us tonight."

"Thank you for squeezing us in. This is my date, Nichole."

"Hello. You're in for a treat tonight. The snacks will start shortly along with your wine. I hope you enjoy your time with us."

"Thank you," Nichole smiles sweetly. The chef walks away and Nichole looks at me, "Date?" she raises her eyebrow, questioning my terminology.

"Well, I couldn't say this is the girl I'm fucking and I thought if I introduced you as my girlfriend you would go running out the door so I took the safe road. What should I call you?"

Nichole smiles, not responding to my question and looking down at the menu, which is a notebook with a pencil that reads *A Field Guide To Lazy Bear*.

We are served an eleven-course meal that starts with snacks and then a tasting menu. Each course is served with a wine pairing making the entire experience extremely unique.

We engage in conversation with the people seated next to us and the night moves along perfectly.

After dinner we walk back to the limo and climb inside.

"So, is this when I get to fuck you in a limo?" Nichole teases grabbing my tie and pulling me close to her.

My mouth tilts up to my cocky smile, "Not yet. I have something else planned first."

"Paul, I told you. You don't have to do this. I'm already going to fuck your brains out."

I kiss her sweetly, "I know. I want to though."

We discuss dinner and all the unique things we tried as the limo drives to Union Square, dropping us off at the Starlight Room located on top of the Sir Francis Drake Hotel. The high-end cocktail lounge sits on the 21st floor with views of Union Square and the rest of San Francisco.

I reserved us a VIP table and we're seated right away. Nichole looks at me as she slides into the circular table. "Paul, really, this is too much. We could have sat at a normal table."

I grab her hand, looking straight into her eyes, softly replying, "I don't know what happened to you in the past that makes you feel like you have to be a bad ass when it comes to guys or to make you feel like you don't deserve a special night. Obviously no one has ever tried to sweep you off your feet. Please let me."

Nichole's face goes flush and after a brief silence she leans in, kissing me on the cheek, whispering, "Thank you."

Sitting back up straight, Nichole looks around the bar and I see a slight look of fear in her eyes. The VIP booth gives us more privacy than the restaurant did and this is definitely more of a real date now. She knots her hands in her lap as she bites her bottom lip.

I reach down, grabbing her hand firmly commanding her to look up at me. I remove my hand from hers and bring my thumb to her mouth pulling her lip out from her teeth. "Don't be scared doll. Just breathe."

I place my hand on her cheek and she slightly leans into my touch as her eyes reach up to meet mine again. A slow smile comes over her face as she lets out a slow ragged breath.

She slowly moves toward me, cuddling up in my arms for a brief moment before the waitress comes over to take our drink order.

We sit there all night, enjoying one another's company while drinking some of the Starlight Room's specialty drinks.

Once back in the limo I look at her asking, "My house or yours?"

Nichole kisses me on the lips, whispering, "Yours."

"Really?" I kiss her back. "So you'll stay the night?"

"Yes, Paul, I will stay the night with you."

As we enter my apartment Nichole starts unzipping her dress seductively walking straight to my bedroom. "I think I owe you a blow job for tonight."

I grab her from behind, pulling her in, whispering in her ear, "I didn't take you out tonight just to make you feel like you had to repay me with sex."

Nichole turns to look at me, giving me a look of confusion.

"Don't get me wrong, I'm going to fuck you silly but I just want you to know that was not my only intention with taking you out tonight."

She wraps her arms around my neck and leans in to kiss my ear before moving down my neck, whispering, "Then why else would you go through all of this trouble?"

I place each of my hands on either side of her face so I can look directly into her eyes, "Nichole, I like you. I haven't liked anyone in awhile. I wanted to spend a night out with you, that's all."

"Paul, you could have showed me that in bed, for free."

"It's not about the money. I want to show you just how special you're becoming to me, outside of my bed. It just felt right. Don't question it." I lean in to kiss her lips softly, "I hope you're feeling the same way."

I can feel heat rise to her face and she looks down, not sure how to respond.

Leaning down, I try to look into her eyes, "Is that ok with you?"

Nichole looks up, "I'm sorry. It's just... I mean... I've never had someone go through so much just to tell me they like me. Paul, I don't date. I've only ever dated one other person and I walked in on him screwing my roommate. I just don't know how all of this is supposed to go."

"Well, now you do. I'm sorry that happened to you. Things make more sense now but don't over think this. Do you feel the same way about me?"

Nichole doesn't answer, looking up to me as her eyes fill with hope and she nods her head *yes*.

I rub my thumb over her bottom lip before leaning down to kiss her softly as I wrap my arms around her and lift her up off the floor a few inches to my height.

I hold her tightly, kissing her before slowly lowering her down back to the floor. "Now, let's go to my room so I can show you how much I like you in my bed," I say as I slap her ass.

Nichole laughs, "There's the man I know," as she runs to my room, begging for me to chase her, which, of course, I do.

Twelve

Allison

My stomach tenses as I approach Alex's building the next day. Squeezing my fists together, I take a deep breath in, determined as I walk up to the building, not wanting what happened with Jacquelyn to ruin my chances with Alex and my new job.

Every day will get easier...

I enter the room to see a group of men dressed in suits. Their age's range from 70 to what I guess to be 30. I smile sweetly as I excuse myself through the crowd and walk up to Holly, the receptionist.

My eyes are big as I look at Holly, tilting my head toward the group, trying to ask who these guys are without saying anything.

Holly turns in her chair so she's facing away from the group, "This is Howard, Dean and Prescott, the law firm you're shooting today. Very boring stuff but the one leaning against the door with the three-day old stubble is cute," she smiles.

I slyly look back to the group to get a good view before raising my eyebrows back to Holly. "Hmm, yeah, not bad. I'll see if I can get him talking for you. Check out if he's married or not."

We smile at each other before I playfully hit her arm and walk back into the studio.

"So our photo shoot is indoors today I take it?" I ask Alex who is setting up lights.

"I know, boring head shots but hey, it pays the bills. I figured you could hone your lighting skills and maybe we could start working toward you being a certified professional photographer. Some of the photos you need to submit can be pretty boring so you might as well get paid while you do it."

"That would be wonderful. Thank you for wanting to help me. I thought it would be years until I even tried."

"You're ready and I would love to help you. Blame it on me being a dad. Marissa let me teach her a little but she wanted to do more motion pictures. I guess it does have some of the same aspects but you know, kids don't want to work with their dad. It's not *cool*."

I laugh, "Yeah, I get it. Well I'm honored you would want to help me. It's her loss."

We work together setting up the background and lights before calling each lawyer back for their individual headshot.

What could have been a very simple and boring photo shoot, Alex has turned in to a master learning session for me. We work on getting the lighting just right on three-quarters of the face so the shadows are the perfect darkness. I soak in all the information Alex is giving me and love the technical process to produce the perfect picture.

We gather the group for their group shot and after everyone leaves I walk over to the computer, anxious to view the photos.

As they are loading in the computer, Alex walks over congratulating me, "You did really good today. How do you feel about it? Did it get easier with each person?"

"It did. I'm excited to see them. I can't thank you enough for taking the time to really show me."

"I told you. I'm glad to help."

The photos come up on the screen one at a time and Alex smiles, "These are great. Good job."

"Thank you!" I'm literally jumping up and down in my seat.

"Hey, I don't have anything scheduled for tomorrow, how about we head out and take some shots to build your portfolio. I hear the beach will actually be sunny for a change," he laughs. "Why don't you see if you can get your sister and Charlie to model for you?"

"Really? That would be amazing. I'm sure they would do it. Thank you."

"Great. Keep me posted if they can't do it and I'll meet you at one out at Ocean Beach. I'll bring all the gear, don't worry about anything."

Charlie, Nichole and I pull up in Charlie's Mustang to a sunny Ocean Beach.

"Wow, what a beautiful day," Nichole says looking around.

"Yeah, it couldn't be more perfect. Thank you guys again for coming out to do this," I say.

Charlie wraps his arms around me, "You know we would do anything for you. Both of us," he smiles to Nichole.

"Yeah, yeah, yeah, I love you... Ok, let's go take some photos," Nicole says as she starts to walk to the beach.

Alex has already scoped a spot and is setting up some lights as we approach. "Hey Alex, how can I help?" I ask.

"Hey guys. Glad you could make it. It's great that you're willing to help Allison." He reaches his hand out to Charlie and then Nichole.

"We're glad to help. What's the plan? What are we shooting?" Charlie asks Alex.

"I don't know. You have to ask the lead photographer of the shoot that question. It's all up to her, I'm just the assistant today."

I tense up; I didn't know I would be doing *everything* today. After a second, a small smile covers my face. This is what I've dreamed of for years. Here is my chance to do what I want. The idea makes my heart flutter and my hands tingle with excitement.

"Ok, I saw a volleyball net set up just a ways down. Let's head down to get some shots of Charlie playing. Then we can get Nichole lying on a towel, sunbathing. Then, oh yeah, we can get Nichole in the water, maybe about knee high with the water splashing around her."

"Sounds like a plan," Alex claps his hands together. "Here, Charlie, help me move these lights."

We walk to the Volleyball net and start to set up the lights. I look at Charlie, "Hey baby," I say as sweet as possible. "I want you all tattered and sweaty..." I raise my eyebrows as I slap his ass. "Now go run."

He laughs, holds his hand up to his forehead in a salute and says, "Yes ma'am," as he winks and heads off to run down the beach.

Charlie is gone for about fifteen minutes and when he returns the shot is all set up. He's breathing heavy and he removes his shirt. The longer he stands there the more his body covers in a deliciously sexy sweat and it's exactly the look I want.

I look at him, reaching out and touching his chest, "Oh yeah, perfect baby." I smile, lifting up to kiss his lips.

Charlie grabs me, pulling me into him, rubbing his sweaty body all over me. I laugh, fighting him off, "No, I need you sweaty. Don't rub it off on me."

He whispers in my ear, "But I like to rub it out on you." He raises his eyebrows as he lets me go.

I hit his chest, "Get to work. Go look gorgeous over there for me."

We set up the shot and take photos of him spiking the ball, reaching out long, displaying the sweat dripping down his chest and his board shorts that hang just a little too low.

"Wow, all we need is some dog tags and we'd have our very own Maverick," Nichole yells out making everyone laugh.

I nod my head up and down, "I know. The exact look I was going for." I smile looking back into the camera to take another shot.

Next we get Nichole lying on the beach, looking sexy as ever, of course. She wears a black string bikini with her hair lying long covering her shoulders. I set her in multiple poses, standing up, lying down, all very sexy.

"Ok, let's get you in the water," I guide Nichole on the next shot.

She enters the water to knee height as I click photos of the water crashing in behind her.

"Nichole, dunk your head so your hair is wet and slicked back. Go slow so I can get you coming out of the water, too."

Nichole does as she's told and I smile, happy with what I'm seeing.

Alex walks up behind me, "You should get the two of them together, in the water."

I turn swiftly to Alex with a blank look on my face, kind of surprised he suggested it.

"Hey, I get it. Remember, I started off shooting my wife. I had to see her with all kinds of guys but it's just the business. And if you don't think you can trust him at least you know you can trust her. She's your sister," he laughs.

I fake a weak smile. *Ugh. I know I can trust both of them but really? Photos of them together? I know, sex sells but God, my boyfriend and my sister…*

I shake my head trying to act professional. "You're probably right." I turn to Charlie. "Would you mind getting in the water with Nichole?"

Charlie looks at me, "Really?"

"Yeah, it will be fine. I'll direct you as to what I want you to do."

Charlie timidly walks to the water shrugging his shoulders to Nichole. Nichole laughs, "Come here sexy."

"Ok Nichole…" I yell out as a warning.

"Oh, get over yourself." She looks at Charlie, "Don't get me wrong, you're sexy and you know it but I like my bad boy."

Charlie laughs, "Hey, Paul's got nothing on me."

"Ok you guys. Charlie, I need you wet, too. Then put your arms around Nichole's waist."

Charlie dunks under the water then pulls Nichole into him. They both laugh in an awkward moment. He lifts his eyebrows to Nichole making her laugh even more.

"Ok, this is supposed to be sexy, not funny," I yell out.

Nichole calms her face and looks up to Charlie. "It's ok if I just envision you as Paul right?"

"I'm not sure about that. Don't molest me like you do him," he laughs.

She grabs his ass, jokingly, "Come on."

"Nichole…" I yell out.

They both turn to me and laugh. "Ok, ok, let's be serious." Charlie wraps his hands around her waist and pulls her in closer, looking into her eyes.

Nichole tries to hold back her laughter, trying to be professional.

"That's good, just a little closer," I guide them. "Good. Now Charlie, take your pointer finger and rub it down her jaw line, looking into her eyes."

He does and I look through the viewfinder loving the photo I'm creating but hating seeing the two people together that are creating it. I take a deep breath, pushing my feelings to the side.

Alex places his hand on my shoulder, knowing I need the mental support to get through this. I look at him in an un-said thank you.

"Good. Now Charlie, rub your thumb along her bottom lip. Yes, just like that. Nichole, look up at him more. Look into his eyes."

"What the FUCK?" Paul appears on the beach behind us and he's raging mad.

Nichole and Charlie instantly let go of each other looking at Paul.

I turn around, "Paul. I'm sorry. It's just photos. Believe me, I don't like seeing it either but they're great photos. I'm just trying to build my portfolio."

"Just photos my ass. He had his hands all over her!"

Charlie starts to walk out of the water toward Paul. "Hey man, I promise. Nothing was going on."

"Bro, you stay there. Don't come toward me." Paul closes his eyes, breathing for a second, trying to calm down, then throws his hands up, "I'm out of here."

"Paul, no, wait!" Nichole yells after him.

He's a good distance away and is walking faster than Nichole. He hops on his bike before Nichole can reach him and speeds away. Nichole turns back to the group wrapping her arms around her body as she starts to shake.

Charlie and I walk toward her. "Nichole, I'm so sorry," I say reaching out to her.

"It's ok. I mean, he has to get used to seeing me like this. This is my profession and I'm not giving it up for him. Screw him anyway. This is why I don't date. He just walked away from me. We're done."

I know she's just trying to put on a front but I don't want to call her out on it. Not now. "Ok, I think we got enough for today. Let's call it a wrap. Thank you again for doing this for me."

"No prob, sis." She looks at Charlie. "Damn man, your eyes are something else. You're lucky you're with my sister." She tries to lighten the mood with her give-a-shit attitude.

Charlie laughs, wrapping his arms around me from behind. "Yup, I'm all hers."

Charlie

Once we get home I head straight up to Paul's place but he's not there. I pull out my phone to text him:

Hey bro. Please don't be mad. It was only a photo shoot. I swear.

FUCK MAN. I KNOW. I JUST HAVE OTHER SHIT ON MY MIND AND I LOST MY COOL.

It's all good. Where are you? I'm at your place.

I'M AT THE BAR. COME DOWN FOR A DRINK.

Cool. Be right there.

I walk into the bar around the corner from our house to see Paul sitting alone at the bar with a half empty bottle of beer in front of him. I don't say anything to him as I sit down, ordering a beer from the bartender. Paul looks up at me, sighing before looking back down.

"You ok man? What's up?"

He sighs again. "Yeah. I'm ok. Lost my cool though. Fuck, what is this girl doing to me?"

I laugh, "I hear you bro. Look at us, sitting here, both of us with girlfriends, sisters at that."

Paul smirks, "No shit." He looks down and plays with the label of his beer bottle as he confesses. "I'm not sure what happened. I have a lot of other things on my mind," he pauses. "But I know you love Allison. I know it was just a photo shoot but yet I saw you, with your thumb on her bottom lip and I just lost it. I only left cause I felt stupid for losing my cool. I've never had that reaction before." He looks up at me, "This really blows."

I laugh again, hitting his back, "Now you get it. You have it bad, too."

Paul looks up at me smirking while shaking his head in disbelief. "Yeah, now she's pissed though. She's sent me a few text messages bitching, saying modeling is her profession and she won't give it up like you gave up your gig for Allison and I would never ask her to do that. How do I admit that I was jealous without sounding like a pussy?"

"My best advice, if you really want her… Lay it all out there. Believe me.

Secrets get you nowhere. Obviously you want to be with her. Tell her you're sorry, you fucked up, it won't happen again," I smirk. "It will be ok. I was there. I think she was just as worried about losing you as you were her. She just tries to hide it more. She's into your bad-boy ways, even told me so before you showed up acting all bad ass."

Paul laughs, "Jeez, thanks."

PAUL

I power off my phone right before I knock on Nichole's door. My stomach turns with nerves, still not sure how much I'm going to tell her. She answers the door, surprised to see me standing there.

"Why are you even here?" Nichole snaps at me. "I told you. I'm a model. I will have many more photo shoots like that. This is why I don't date. Just leave."

I stop her from slamming the door. "No, Nichole. I won't let you do that. Look, I know I fucked up. I'm sorry. I've never done this either. I'll admit it. I got jealous. I got so fucking jealous. I lost my mind. It's not a feeling I'm used to and I didn't handle it right."

I reach out to grab her hand as I look down. She doesn't pull away from me so I look up to meet her eyes, "I'm sorry. I like you, maybe a little too much for my own good. Do you forgive me?"

Nichole snatches her hand away from me. "Why are you even doing this? I know there's someone else. Don't think I didn't notice how you turn your phone off when you're around me. Show me. Is it even on right now? What happen to 'I only fuck one person at a time' huh Paul?"

Fuck.

My eyes go big as I search for words but come up with nothing.

Nichole goes on, "I saw it Paul. When I programmed my number in your phone. You had missed calls from someone named Beth. I blew it off but the more I paid attention the more I saw you always turning off your phone. Why? Is that so I wouldn't know who else you're messing around with? Well, I know. And your silence proves it. So just leave."

She turns on her heel to leave me standing outside but I grab for her, quickly swinging her around pulling her into me. "It's not what you think. I promise."

"Whatever Paul. I told you, you were just a good fuck and now it's over. Just leave."

"No Nichole, wait." I pull out my phone from my back pocket and power it on. "I'm telling you. It's not what you think. Beth is definitely not someone I sleep with or even want to have any kind of relationship with. It's someone I don't even want in my life but unfortunately sometimes you don't get to decide who is in or out of your life."

I show her my phone that displays 105 unread text messages and 30 voicemails. "See, I have not listened to or read any of her messages. I'm telling you, I don't want anything to do with her."

She doesn't say a word, just stares at my phone and back to me. My eyes start to sag, ashamed of what's going on.

She whispers, "Then who is she? Why don't you just block her phone number? Or at least delete the messages?"

I release her from my arms and turn around, running my fingers through my hair, whispering, "She's my mother."

"Your mother?"

"Yeah. My mother. The woman who gave birth to me. The woman I want nothing to do with. Who I have tried so hard to rid from my life and make something of myself just to get away from her and everything she represents." I still have my back to her, afraid to face her. "I don't want to listen to what she has to say but I can't bring myself to delete the messages."

"I don't understand."

"Fuck," I throw my fists around in a swooping motion in front of me. "Why did she have to come back now?" I whisper more to myself than Nichole.

She walks up behind me, placing her hands on my back. "What is it? Why don't you want her in your life?"

I take a deep breath and finally look at her. "Nichole, I didn't have the best upbringing. I was serious when I told you I have worked hard for everything I have. My mom has no idea who my father is. She's a crack addict whore who has been in and out of my life for years. I would get taken away from her for various reasons and live in foster care. Then she would clean up and get me back only for the entire process to start over about a year later. She couldn't stay clean and would do anything for a fix when she needed it. Including selling herself and bringing tricks back to our house with me there."

I pause to gauge her reaction before continuing. "If I didn't have the Boys and Girls Club to help me I don't know what I would have done. Vince, the director there, saw the potential in me and helped me with my schoolwork. He introduced me to architecture when he saw me drawing buildings on my notepad. He said I could make it a career and he helped guide me through college scholarship applications. Shit, he even fed me when my mom spent every dime she had on getting high. My goal in life was to be anything but her. I got into Cal Poly on a full scholarship and have worked my ass off to be the best I could possibly be. Without her."

Nichole's eyes fill with tears as she listens to everything I've gone through.

"I haven't heard from her in years. When I first got established and started making good money she found me. I wanted so bad to just rid her from my life but I couldn't. No matter what, she's still my mother. But I wanted to keep her out of my life. So I set her up with an account and said I would pay for her living expenses if she would just leave me alone. Every month $4,000 is transferred from my account to hers to automatically pay her housing, utilities and an account at a local grocery store. That way I don't have to see or do anything. Deep down I can't live with myself knowing she's not taken care of. Even though I want nothing to do with her, I at least know she has a place to live and food on the table."

"So why is she calling you now?"

"I don't know. I can't bring myself to listen to the voicemails. The text messages I have seen just say she needs to talk to me but doesn't say why." I slump my shoulders down in defeat letting out a long sigh.

Nichole walks up to me, so close she's pressing her body against mine. "I'm sorry Paul." She places her hand on my face. "I'm sorry you have to deal with this and I'm sorry I thought you were seeing someone else. Thank you for telling me. Is there anything I can help with?"

I look into her eyes, "Can we just drop it? I really don't want to drag her into my life. My life with you. Do you forgive me for acting like a total ass today?"

Nichole sighs, looking down before replying, "I'm not giving up modeling. This is what I do. You need to be ok with that."

I pull her in closer. "I am ok with that. I love that my phone says 'I'm fucking a model.' I would never ask you to change who you are."

Nichole laughs, "You left that on there? After your client saw it?"

"Hell yeah I did. It's sexy as hell. And I don't care who sees it. I'm proud."

"Ok Paul, but don't fuck up again."

I lean in, kissing her lips sweetly, "I won't, promise." I look back at her, tilting up one eyebrow, "Can we have makeup sex now?"

Nichole laughs, "And here I thought you were getting all soft on me."

"I'm always hard for you." I lean in, kissing her neck before picking her up and running up the stairs.

Thirteen

PAUL

The morning light peeks through the blinds in Nichole's room as I'm wrapped around her lying in bed. She reaches up to touch my face making my eyes slowly open and a small grin grows on my lips.

"I'm sorry, I didn't mean to wake you."

"Hmm, it's ok. Morning." I lean in to kiss her lips gently.

"Morning. I couldn't sleep."

"I'm sorry, were you uncomfortable?"

"No, I was just thinking."

"About what doll?"

"About you. About your mom."

My smile disappears, "Please don't. I didn't want to tell you. It's not your problem to worry about."

"Hey, you're the one who wanted to have sleepovers," she teases. "Maybe if I didn't have you draped all over me while I'm trying to sleep I wouldn't be thinking about you so much."

I smirk, "Ok, my bad." I lean in to kiss her again.

"I think you should listen to the messages."

I sit up, removing my arm that was wrapped around her. "No, Nichole." I prop my arms on my knees I pulled up close under the sheets as I run my fingers through my hair. "I told you, don't worry about it. Let me deal with it."

Nichole leans up, putting her arm on mine and leaning her head on my shoulder. "Please let me help you. I'll listen with you." She turns around to pick up my phone from the nightstand and hands it to me.

I give her a grim stare then look down to my phone without grabbing it from her.

"Hey, you're the one that started this whole thing. I just wanted to fuck. Now you have me caring what happens to you."

I let out a quick laugh grabbing the phone from her. "So this is how you show me? Making me do something I don't want to do?"

"No, I show you by letting you stay the night wrapped around me. This is just an added bonus," she smiles.

I look down to my phone and power it on. "She hasn't called in the last few days. Maybe she got what she needed from someone else."

When my phone powers on completely there is a missed call from a 415 number that came in around two in the morning.

"Is that her?" Nichole asks as she looks over my shoulder at my phone.

"No, not sure who that is."

I click the voicemail and put it on speakerphone so Nichole can hear as well.

"Hello. This message is for Paul Foust. This is San Francisco General Hospital. We have Beth Foust here and she says you are her emergency contact. Can you please give us a call back?"

"Fuck me." I throw the phone down on the bed.

Nichole takes a sharp breath in, wrapping her arms around me tighter. "Are you going to call them back?"

"Fuck," I look at her, "Do I have a choice?"

"I'm sorry Paul. Do you want me to call them back?"

"No," I snap at her before looking back down to my phone and picking it back up.

"Are you going to listen to the other messages first?"

I take a deep breath and scroll to the first message she left on my phone, hitting play and leaving it on speakerphone.

Beth's shaky voice plays over the speakerphone. "Paul, it's your mother…" Long pause. "Can you call me sweetheart?"

My jaw tightens at the sound of her voice as I hit delete and play the next one.

"Paul son. I'd love to talk to you. Please call me back."

Then the next.

"I could really use a phone call back, son."

The next.

"Why aren't you calling me back son? I am your mother…"

Next.

"Paul, I really need someth… I mean, I'd love to hear your voice. Please call me back."

Next.

"Son. Don't you love your mother anymore? Call me baby."

My expression hardens as my mother's voice grows in desperation. There are twelve more messages with every message getting a little more needy. The worst one came in at three in the morning a couple of weeks ago.

"Look baby. Mommy needs a, uh, um, you to call me back. Please baby. I'm begging." Her voice is shaky and moving from high to low pitches.

The next morning she called again. "Hi son! Wow I love hearing your voice on your voicemail. You sound so sophisticated and manly. My boy all grown up. Look, sorry for the calls. I'm allllll goooooood noooow," she says giggling into the phone. "Love you, baby."

"Fuck. She's high as a kite…" I grumble staring at my phone.

Nichole holds me tighter placing a small kiss on my cheek. I can't bring myself to look at her but when she kissed me I felt the tightness in my chest loosen instantly.

I hit play to the next message that came in two days after the last one. Her voice is back to shaky and needy and the entire process starts over with her begging for me to call and each call getting worse until the call comes where I can tell she got her fix. In every call she plays the guilt card by calling me son and reminding me she is my mother.

Nichole wipes a tear that fell down her check and I turn to her. "No, please don't cry. I don't want you affected by this. I don't want you crying over my problem."

"Paul I'm sorry. I'm just in shock ok. I've never known anyone addicted to drugs. Just listening to these voicemails is really overwhelming and the thought of you having to deal with this all of your life is a little much for me to take in."

I just shake my head looking down, "You have no idea."

"Are you going to call the hospital back?"

I snap at her, "As I already said, do I have a fucking choice?"

Her eyes get big at my response and I look back down, running my fingers through my hair. "Look, I'm sorry. I didn't want anyone to know. Charlie doesn't even know. I don't want people to feel sorry for me."

"I know…" she says as she gets up to give me space to make the phone call.

I put my feet on the ground and hunch over, placing my elbows on my knees, running my fingers through my hair and I hit the call button and hold it up to my ear.

"San Francisco General Hospital, how may I direct your call?"

"Hello, Beth Foust is a patient there. I have a missed phone call from someone saying they were trying to reach me."

"Yes, I see she is a patient here. Let me transfer you to the nurse's station. I see here that she can't accept phone calls at this time."

I look up in frustration, dropping my head back, "Thank you."

The phone beeps a few times and someone answers, "Hello, is this Paul Foust?"

"Yes, I hear Beth is a patient there. What happened?"

"Yes sir. I'm afraid she's in pretty bad shape. She was found in an alley beaten badly over in Hunters Point."

"Fuck. Was she prostituting?"

"Sir, I'm not sure of the details. You'll have to talk to the police about that. She's heavily sedated due to the detox process. Before we had to sedate her she gave us your number as a contact person. Are you able to come in to help fill out paperwork?"

I sigh, running my hand over my face. "Fine, I'll be there as soon as I can."

Nichole is standing at the door holding a glass of water. I turn to look at her as she sits down on the bed next to me handing me the glass. "Everything ok?"

"No. She's in the hospital, pretty beat up and going through detox. They found her in an alley. My guess is she was prostituting again. Fuck, maybe I should have called her back. Maybe then she wouldn't have sold herself to get high."

"No, Paul. Don't say that. You can't support your mom's drug habit. This is not your fault. She's a grown woman who can make her own choices. By what you have said you already do enough for her."

I look at her with pain in my eyes as I try to give her a smile. "Thanks, baby. I have to head to the hospital."

I get up and Nichole grabs my hand stopping me. "Can I come?"

I shrug, "If you want to, I guess."

We walk into the hospital hand-in-hand. After I fill out the necessary paperwork we're shown to her room and stand at the door, not walking in. I shake my head then look down to Nichole's hand ashamed. "Look, I'm not sure if you should come in. I don't want to put you through this."

"Stop Paul. I'm going in. Come on." She pulls on my hand as she moves the curtain to reveal a frail woman lying on a hospital bed with a tube down her throat, her arm and leg are in a cast and her left eye is swollen to the size of a baseball all black and blue.

I stop and grip Nichole's hand tighter as my breath catches. Nichole looks at me, wrapping her other hand around mine as she steps in front of me to look in my eyes. "You can do this."

I look back to her, giving her a small nod as we walk further into the room. A nurse follows us in asking, "Are you family?"

"Yes, I'm… her son," I look down to the floor. "Can you tell me what happened?"

"Well, she was found in an alley at Hunters Point around eleven last night. As you can tell she was beaten pretty badly. Looks like she is going to survive but she's going through a massive detox so we had to sedate her because of her injuries. We don't want to keep giving her morphine for pain when she's detoxing so it's best if we sedate her. Do you know what kind of drugs she uses?"

I shake my head as I clench my jaw tightly. "She should be clean. Dammit. Who knows with her? You name it she's done it. I have no clue what her current drug of choice is." I get up to walk out the door. "You have my number. There is no need for me to be here right now. If she wakes up give her this." I pull a note from my back pocket and walk out of the room.

Nichole looks at the nurse who is just as stunned as she is I'm sure, then runs to catch up with me. "What was that note?"

I don't stop to reply, just keep walking, determined to leave the hospital. Once I'm outside I finally reply, "Fuck her. I'm done. I told her if she doesn't go to rehab, and stay in rehab this time, I am cutting her off completely."

"Paul…"

"Don't do this Nichole. This is why I didn't want you to know. I can only be pushed so far." I look away ashamed. "Don't think less of me, please. I've tried. I really have."

Nichole stops me, holding my face in her hands, "Hey. Stop. This is not the Paul I know. Don't look away from me. I know you've tried. I will never think less of you for having a mother like this. I'm blown away that you support her at all. Call me heartless but I would have kicked her to the curb years ago. Don't beat yourself up over this."

"Fine, can we just go?"

"Do you want to go back to my place and fuck like animals? Will that get your mind off of this mess? Cause that I can do, I'm good at that." She lifts her eyebrows to me smiling her sexy smile.

I grab her ass, pulling her close to me, slamming her against my hard body. "I knew I was keeping you around for a reason. Hell yes that will make things better. You're my type of girl you know that?"

"Well then let's go big boy," Nichole says over her shoulder as she walks toward my bike with a sexy grin on her face.

Before she puts on her helmet she reaches out and hugs me. That's it. No smart ass comment. No kissing. No sexual innuendos. Just a simple hug but let me tell you, this hug is knocking me to my knees. I've never felt this small simple act before.

A hug, from a woman, who truly cares. It's amazing.

I've sensed she's starting to feel the same way about me as I am about her and this proves it.

Something special is definitely happening here.

We step inside my place with the air around us feeling different. I know she senses it too because she's not acting like her ravage, sex kitten self. She's definitely not being shy but not as nonchalant as before about us being together.

She walks toward me with a different look in her eyes and I'd be lying if I said my cock didn't go from soft to rock hard real quick.

As she approaches I place my hand on her face whispering, "Thank you for going with me today."

She leans her head into my hand, something she's never done before, as her eyes close for just a brief moment. Then she opens them looking straight at me. She doesn't reply but her kiss sure does.

My God this woman is unbelievable. I'm not sure what's happening here but I definitely don't want it to stop.

Our kiss is so slow and I swear I feel her body shiver with every pass of my tongue. I wrap my arms around her waist, lifting her slightly and walking toward my room, never breaking our kiss.

I lay her down, slowly lifting her shirt over her head before kissing down her neck to her breasts and stomach. Nothing is said but I feel it. She is officially mine and I'm going to love on every single inch of her.

She arches her back and hips, signaling me to remove her jeans and I'm her huckleberry, more than happy to oblige her command.

Even just the simple task of removing her jeans feels different now. Nothing is rushed. It's like we both want to savior every second and make it last longer than the second before.

I pull off my own shirt, leaning between her legs, kissing up from her tight stomach to her soft lips. I rub my fingers on the outside of her thin lace panties as I capture her moan with my mouth.

So. Fucking. Good. My. God.

Her fingers reach to undo my belt and jeans so I pull back to remove them completely, along with her panties.

I stare at her, lying on my bed, in disbelief that I'm caring for the woman I'm about to make love to.

Whoa, wait, did I really just think that?

Fuck me, I did and I'm actually ok with it.

Nichole must have sensed my ah-ha moment because a small smile grew on her face as she reached up, placing her soft hand on my face and this time it's my turn to lean into her simple touch.

"Nichole…"

"Shh," she places her finger over my lips. "Don't say anything."

I lean in, kissing her again, placing the tip of my cock against her wet entrance.

"I want you Nichole."

"Take me then."

"No," I say through kisses on her neck. "I want the entire experience. Something I've never done with any other woman."

"I told you. Take me then. I want it, too. I'm on the pill."

Oh. Fuck. Yes.

I thrust into her and I swear I see stars.

She feels so fucking amazing. I could blow my load any minute so I pull back, taking a deep breath before kissing her and slowing pushing back in.

We moan into each other's mouth and I'm so glad to see she's feeling it, too. The most incredible feeling I've ever had and she's right underneath me feeling me the way I'm feeling her.

I never want this to stop. Here I just had the worst day of my life turn into the best day of my life. All because of Nichole.

The thought alone increases the intensity I'm feeling and I can't get enough. Pumping into her, making her scream out my name before I kiss her hard, bringing her to her breaking point as she shatters around me.

I grunt my own release. Right inside her and it feels so amazing. So real. Like I've never wanted anything else.

She's mine and I am hers.

Fourteen

Dectective O'Brien

It's late but I can't seem to break this case and it's killing me. I'm at home looking over everything I have that is covering the entire length of my dining room table. Frustrated, I pick up the background checks I just ran on Diane Hayes, Jacquelyn Sanders and Charles Ashley.

I read:

Name: Diane Marie Hayes. Maiden name: Devine. Born: April 5, 1953 in San Francisco. Husband: Kevin Hayes. He's an attorney. She's a housewife. Lives in the Marina District in the City. They have two girls together, Nichole and Allison.

How did she meet Jacquelyn again?

I flip through my notepad. *Oh, at the gym. Why did Jacquelyn belong to a gym in the City? I should check out this gym.*

I write a note on my notepad.

Next I pick up Charlie's background check. Name: Charles Thomas Ashley. Born: January 26, 1987 in Fairfield, California. Not married. No kids. He's a customer service representative for Livingston, Inc. *What is that again?* I write in my notepad to look into the business he works for.

Next is Jacquelyn's. Name: Jacquelyn Ann Sanders. Maiden name: Smith. Born: July 20, 1973. Not employed. Holds patent for green screen technology used in movies. Receives royalties from patent. Net worth: $50 million. *Whoa. Damn. Ok, there's a motive right there.*

I put down the paper and tap my finger on the desk, looking over all the other evidence as my mind starts to wander when my wife, Sandy, walks into the room.

"How's it coming Sam?" Sandy asks while rubbing my back.

I sigh, "I got nothing. Obviously they're hiding something but what?"

"I'm sure you'll figure it out. You always do."

I look over to my wife of 43 years with nothing but love. No matter how stressful my life gets with my job she's always been my driving force.

She simply amazes me.

The way she's raised our four kids practically on her own. I mean, of course I was there but with my job I wasn't the reliable one. She was. I missed birthdays, recitals or baseball games because I was called off to work another case. She offered our kids the stability we all needed and I love her more today than the day I married her.

"Did you hear the great news we got today?" she says smiling from ear to ear.

"No," I look at my phone to see if I have a missed call or text and I notice I do, from my son, Nick. I shake my head, saddened that I'm so busy I miss important calls from my boy. "What's the news?"

"Leah's pregnant again," she smiles as her eyes light up.

I smile in return. "That's wonderful. How many grandkids will that make now?" I laugh, shaking my head.

She smiles as she proudly says, "Nine. Can you believe it?"

I sigh, smiling, "No, that's amazing." I grab her hand before leaning over to kiss her forehead as I get up from the table. "I have to go grab something from my car."

"I'm going to shower then go to bed. Don't stay up too late though, ok?"

I give her a hug, "I won't hun. Goodnight."

Fifteen

Allison

Halloween is coming up and Charlie and I, along with Nichole and Paul, plan on going to the annual Halloween party, Masquerotica, held at the Factory on Harrison Street, which is right around the corner from Charlie and Paul's apartment. The event took over for the famous Exotic Erotic Ball after it ended its thirty-year run and the new event has held up to the vision of the original ball.

The costumes never disappoint, as everyone is dressed as creative and as sexual as they can be. Though nudity is not allowed, people push the limits with pasties and very sheer material. It's a true San Francisco party in all its freak style.

We all meet at Paul's place to do shots before we go.

I'm dressed as a sexy butterfly. My corset style outfit has blue and black feather wings sticking out from the front breast and hip portion sucking my waist in the middle. It's a body suit that resembles a full-length bathing suit, leaving my legs bare except for the sheer, thigh-high black stockings. I choose long black gloves running up my arms to complete my outfit.

Charlie is dressed more simply and focuses more on the color to match my costume, wearing black pants that hang off his hips showing his sexy abs and his stunning V-line pointing to what I know is pure heaven, along with a black and blue, feathered bowtie and eye mask to match my wings.

"Goddamn girl!" I yell when I first see Nichole wearing a short, strapless, black latex outfit with her ass and boobs barely covered. She has a silver and black necktie tied around her neck that is tucked into her breasts and her thigh-high latex looking stiletto boots round out her outfit.

"Don't be jealous just because I can pull it off," she teases.

"Oh jeez, your head has gotten even bigger since you started hanging out with Paul," I laugh back.

"How can you talk shit? She looks fucking hot. I already had to take her out of the outfit once before you guys got here," Paul interrupts as he grabs Nichole's ass.

Paul matches Nichole's look wearing black jeans, a black button-up dress top with small silver squares and his cuffs rolled up revealing black latex gloves pulled up to his elbows and a black latex eye mask to match.

"Hey, she can pull it off, no doubt, I was just shocked to see her try in the first place."

"Thanks sis, you look pretty hot yourself. And Charlie… Look at those abs," she reaches out to rub his stomach.

"Hey, hey, hey now," Paul laughs.

"Oh stop it Paul, you know I'm not trying to hit on my sister's man," Nichole hits his stomach. "Or anyone else for that matter," she reaches up to kiss him.

"That's right," he smiles.

"Ok you guys, let's do shots and get out of here," Charlie pipes in handing everyone shot glasses. "Here's to a fun, safe night out. Happy Halloween."

We all say, "Happy Halloween," in unison as we take our shot and head out.

The party is already well underway and everyone is drunk and having a great time. We all grab another drink as we people watch and check out everyone's crazy costumes, before heading out to dance and start our night of Halloween fun.

The drinks are flowing and the crowd is getting looser with each passing minute. The four of us are standing around drinking when an older woman stops, wrapping her arms around Charlie screaming, "Oh, Mr. Ashley! Where have you been?"

The woman runs her hands all over his bare stomach and chest. She is obviously drunk and doesn't notice or seem to care that I am standing right there.

She starts kissing Charlie and rubbing her body tightly against his before Charlie pulls her back, "Gina. Stop. I'm here with someone."

The woman is stunned that he stopped her from kissing him and she looks at me, "Oh honey, you know we all share him. Ohhh, maybe you can join us. You're a sexy little thing," she grabs me, pulling me in, trying to kiss me.

I yank myself out of her grip.

"No, Gina. I quit. This is my girlfriend," Charlie yells.

"Girlfriend?!" Gina throws her head back laughing. "You lucky bitch. I had to pay to fuck this fine ass." She leans down to slap Charlie's ass.

I'm mortified and turn to run away when Nichole jumps up to get in Gina's face, "Look bitch! He said he quit and now he's with my sister. You need to back the fuck up!"

Gina laughs, backing up, "Ok, ok." She looks at Charlie, "I'll miss you Mr. Ashley," and she blows him a kiss.

I turn to run away and they follow until I run into the women's bathroom. I sit in a bathroom stall, crying. "Allison?" Nichole knocks on the door.

"Nichole, give me a minute."

"Hey, I know that totally sucked and I know you…" she pauses, "um, I mean… shit, what can I say?"

I sigh, "Jeez, thanks Nic. That was, um, very reassuring…"

Nichole laughs, "Hey, I may have a boyfriend now but I'm still me. Come on, come out of there."

I wipe my eyes and open the door. Nichole wraps her arms around me, "You ok girl?"

"No!" I give her an are-you-kidding-me look.

"Hey, you should be proud. That woman was jealous you don't have to pay to fuck him."

"Nichole, really, you're not helping."

Nichole laughs, "Sorry, just trying to be real. Hey, it's his past. Unfortunately things like that are going to happen. But really, you should be proud. He gave it all up for you. I don't know any guy who would do that. Paul says all the time that he's shocked he gave it all up."

"I know, it still just sucks. Especially after what happened with his last client I met."

"I know. But hey, this one wanted to do you, not kill you. That's a huge upgrade."

I shake my head, laughing, "Nichole, you really are too much."

"I know. That's why you love me. Now, can we go back out there? I'm sure Charlie is about to lose his mind."

I fix my makeup and turn to leave the bathroom. Charlie is standing right at the door, anxiously waiting for me to come out.

"Allison," he wraps his arms around me, "Please, don't be mad. I swear I want nothing to do with her or anything from my past. Please believe me." Charlie is desperate and rambling on and on for me to forgive him.

"Charlie, it's ok. I'm ok."

"You are?" He looks into my eyes, "Are you sure? I'm so sorry," he leans in to kiss me.

"I know, baby. I know. I think I want to go home though."

"Yeah, of course. Let's go." He looks to Nichole and Paul, "We're heading home, do you guys want to go or stay?"

Nichole and Paul look at each other and shrug, "I'm not quite ready to go," Nichole replies as she grabs Paul, "Come dance with me some more." She leans over to kiss me on my cheek, "Love you girl. Cheer up. Go fuck his brains out and think of all the jealous women out there."

"Nichole, again, you're not helping."

Nichole winks at me as they walk away, leaving us alone.

"Baby, are you sure you're ok?"

"Yes, Charlie. Just take me home," I grab his hand holding on to his arm.

As we walk home I wrap my arms tightly around my body, shielding myself from the cold and the emotions running through me. Charlie swings his arm around me, pulling me close and keeping me warm as we walk in silence.

Once back at the apartment, I take my costume off and hop in the shower without saying a word. The hot water flows down my face making tears start to fall as I let go of everything I was holding in, letting the water fall all around me.

Charlie enters the bathroom already naked and steps into the shower, engulfing my body from behind. I don't move but welcome his arms that hold me together. I cry even harder as he stands silently embracing me.

After a moment he kisses my head, "Allison, please don't cry. I love you and only you. I'm so sorry about my past. If I could change it all I would, in a heartbeat."

I finally turn to look at him, "I know Charlie, that's why I didn't want you to see me cry. I'll get there. It's just hard."

"I know baby. It kills me to see you like this." He leans down to kiss me which becomes all-consuming fast as we're lost in the intensity of the situation and the one thing we can't deny, our love for each other.

Sixteen

Allison

"Christmas is next week and you still haven't spoken to your mom, Allison... You know it will kill her if you ignore her over Christmas, too," Charlie points out.

"I don't care," I say as I walk by, brushing off the subject.

"But Allie, Nichole told me that you guys have a Christmas tradition of getting together Christmas Eve to decorate your tree and eat popcorn and oranges together. She's going to your parent's and she's bringing Paul. Do you really want to miss out on your family tradition just because you're upset with your mother? What about your dad and your sister?"

"You're my family now. Let's start our own family tradition, like we did with Thanksgiving. I loved cooking all day with you." I try to sway Charlie my way.

"Allison, of course we're family, you have no idea how much that means to me to be able to say that, but I don't want you to leave your actual family behind. Especially..."

I stop him, "Hey, don't go there. You can't compare the two."

"Allison, I just want to see you put all of this behind us. You need to forgive her eventually. You said it yourself that 'everything happens for a reason.' So do you really believe that? Or do you not practice what you preach?"

"Charlie, that's not fair. This is different."

"Is it? I mean, if you truly believe that then this baby happened for a reason. And you came into my life for a reason, too. I have to believe that. And I hope you do, too."

Charlie is sitting on the bar stool at the kitchen counter and I walk up between his legs, wrapping my arms around his neck. "Charlie, I told you, I need time. I'm coming around to the idea but let me get over the baby idea first, then I can deal with my mom. I just thank God I don't have to deal with the crazy woman birthing your child. That would push me over the edge," I joke.

Charlie tenses up and I feel the tightness in his shoulders. "Whoa, what was that?"

Charlie tries to blow it off, "What?" he looks to me shrugging his shoulders.

"Charlie, if there is one thing I have learned about you in the past few months it is that you're a terrible liar. What aren't you telling me?"

Charlie moves to sit up and walk to the kitchen, "I don't know what you're talking about. I'm just trying to figure out Christmas."

I grab his arm, stopping him from walking away from me, "Charlie, look at me. Why did you tense up like that? I felt it. Don't act like I didn't."

"I just want you to have your family back. I know you were close to them before all of this happen."

"No Charlie. It was something else. Wait," I try to re-think what just happened. "You were sitting here, your arms around my waist talking about everything happening for a reason. Then you mentioned the baby and you were still calm. I said I was coming around to the idea more then, wait, when I mentioned the crazy woman you tensed up. Why Charlie? Why did you tense up?"

Charlie turns around, digging in the refrigerator, and I know it's just to avoid making eye contact with me. I walk up to the refrigerator, closing it so Charlie is forced to face me. "Have you gone to the hospital lately? Is there something you aren't telling me?"

"I did go actually," he is uplifted a little and smiles as he says, "I... we should be able to find out the sex of the baby the week after Christmas."

I tilt my head, squinting my eyes, "That's great, Charlie, but that's not what made you tense. What else did you learn?"

Charlie sighs loudly, "Ok Allison, you're right. You need to remember that the odds of this happening are really 50/50 so please don't jump to conclusions."

"Ok Charlie, you're freaking me out. What's going on?"

"They've been doing studies and comparing her case to other similar cases and there was one other case where..." he reaches to me, placing his hands on either side of my arms, "where the woman woke up from her coma after she gave birth."

I push his hands off of me, "What?! You mean she could live through this?"

"No Allison. Well, I mean, um, there is a small chance. We won't know until the baby is born. She will either come out of it or officially die. They say her body is in limbo."

"Limbo?! And when were you going to tell me?" I storm off into our bedroom.

Charlie runs after me, "Allison please, please don't be mad. I didn't know how to tell you. And there is such a small possibility that she could wake up, I hoped I wouldn't have to tell you. Please don't be mad."

I grab my purse and put on my shoes, "Charlie, I still deserved to know. We can't have secrets between us. Not any more. Look where secrets got us the first time. How can I trust you're telling me everything?"

Charlie kneels down beside me, "Allison, I am. I swear. There are no secrets. I'm just trying to protect you. I didn't want to upset you with something that might not happen."

"That's the problem Charlie. It might actually happen. So what would you have done then? Huh? Say, 'Oops, sorry Allison. I guess she's going to live. Now you can be step-mommy with this psycho.'" I get up, storming out of the room.

"Allison, please, don't leave mad. I wasn't trying to keep it from you."

"But you did Charlie. You did…"

"Don't leave. Not now," Charlie reaches out, holding onto my arm desperately.

"I told you Charlie, time… Let me go."

He lets go of my arm letting me walk away, "Where are you going?"

I take a deep breath in and out, trying to calm my nerves. "I have to go to the studio. Alex wants to look at proofs today. Again, Charlie, just give me time. I have a lot I need to think about."

Charlie steps closer, looking straight into my eyes. "But you'll come back here right?"

"Yes, Charlie, I'll come back here when I'm finished. Unless I bring it up when I get back, please don't. Let me deal with this internally, ok?"

Charlie kisses me softly and pulls back. "Ok, Allison. I love you. I'll be here when you get back. I'll make us dinner."

I turn around and walk out the door, not saying another word.

Our apartment is not far from the studio but I take my time, taking unnecessary turns, slowly walking as I fight tears from flowing.

God, this adds a whole different element to this situation. There is no way I could be a step-mom and have to deal with this woman the rest of my life. But will she come out of it? What if she doesn't? Then I gave up Charlie for no reason. Can I wait till May to find out? I know the longer I stay with him, the harder it will be to walk away.

The thought of walking away makes me physically ill and I have to stop, putting my hands on my knees to calm my breathing and stop the pain building in my chest.

I finally make it to the studio and walk in hoping that looking at proofs will clear my mind for the time being. The receptionist is off today so I walk straight into Alex's office as he sits at the computer looking over proofs.

"Hey Alex," I try to sound happy.

He turns around looking at me, "Hey Allie, everything ok?"

I turn around, fighting more tears as I place my purse on the chair behind me. My voice cracks as I respond, "Yeah, how do the proofs look?"

Alex stands up and walks toward me, placing his hands on my elbows. "Hey, talk to me. What's going on?"

Tears start to fall down my face, "I'm sorry. This is so unprofessional. I should have been more composed before I came inside. I'll be fine."

Alex wipes a tear away from my cheek, "It's ok. Is it Charlie?" his voice a little higher than it should be.

I sigh, "Yes. But it's ok. Just a lot going on."

Alex leans down to look in my eyes, "Allison, it's ok. Talk to me."

"I'm sorry. I don't want to bore you with our drama." *Because you would never believe me and we would be here all day.*

"Allison, are you guys ok? This is the second time you've come in here like this. Does he treat you ok? You know you can talk to me."

"Oh, no, it's nothing like that. Yes, he treats me great."

"Are you sure Allison? I mean, you deserve to be treated like the angel you are."

I look up to him, surprised at what he just said. "I told you, we'll be ok. It's just normal things," I sigh to myself as I say normal.

"Allison I mean it. If you were my girl I would treat you with the upmost respect and make sure you would never feel this way."

My eyes go big. *Whoa, what did he just say?*

I sit silently looking at him. Not sure how to respond.

"I mean it Allison. I would do anything to make your beautiful smile last a lifetime."

Then he leans down and kisses me, holding me tightly by my arms while he shoves his tongue in my mouth.

I'm completely shocked and sit frozen just as the door opens and Charlie walks through holding a dozen roses.

I push away from Alex, wiping my mouth, staring at Charlie as his eyes fill with immense rage.

Charlie throws the flowers on the ground, turning to leave the room without saying a word.

I run to him, grabbing his arm, "Wait Charlie, it's not what you think! Please Charlie, don't leave."

Charlie looks at me, screaming, "It's not what I think? You mean I didn't just walk in on you kissing Alex?"

"No Charlie, let me explain!" I plead.

He looks to Alex who is standing frozen, "You're right, Allison." He walks to Alex and socks him right across the face, knocking him to the ground before turning to walk away.

I try to stop him again, "Let go of me Allison."

"No Charlie, listen to me. I wasn't kissing him."

"Goodbye Allison!"

I gasp, "No, no Charlie! You don't say goodbye."

Charlie looks straight into my eyes, firmly saying, "Goodbye!"

I fall to the floor as Charlie storms out of the room. Alex stands up and walks over to me. He reaches his arm around me and I stand up, yelling at him, "Look what you did! How could you? God, you said I was like a daughter to you. What kind of sick guy are you? I looked up to you. And you're married!"

I grab my purse and run out of the office to try to stop Charlie again.

As I run outside, I see Charlie speed off in his Mustang with a look of death on his face. I fall to my knees again, crying into my hands in the middle of the busy San Francisco street.

Charlie

I drive a few blocks and am stopped by a boom truck putting up a new billboard around Union Square. I look up to see myself. *Are you fucking kidding me right now?*

Before me I see an ad for Guess Seductive Homme cologne displaying the picture of Allison and I wrapped around each other with Allison's neck tilted up and me kissing her neck.

Fuck me.

I turn up the radio already tuned to Live 105 rock station that's playing Rise Against *Savior* right at the middle of the song where the music slows down to a very slow guitar as the singer slowly and calmly yells *I don't hate you.*

I grab my phone, scrolling to my old client, Gina, and clicking the icon to call her.

"Well, Mr. Ashley. That's a name I didn't expect to see on my caller ID. Especially after our little Halloween incident."

"Yeah baby, I'm back. You up for a movie? This one's on the house. I'm in the mood to play."

"Oh, I'm always up to play. What happened? No girlfriend anymore?"

"Fuck her. I'm on my way."

"Can't wait darling."

I hit my head back against my headrest taking a deep breath in as I change the station before pulling into on-coming traffic to get by the boom truck and drive to Gina's.

Allison calls my phone over and over again but I don't want to talk to her so I turn it off and throw it on the seat next to me.

It takes me ten minutes to get to Gina's house in the Sunset and I quickly turn off the car and jump out, trying not to listen to my mind that is yelling at me for what I'm about to do. My jaw is tense and my eyebrows are scrunched close together as my heart rate starts to pound.

Gina opens the door, "Well hello, Mr. Ashley. Looking hot. Come in…"

I grab her firmly, pulling her in and angrily kissing her. Gina loves it and returns the favor as we walk, wrapped around each other toward her room. Gina pushes me down on the bed and starts to unzip my pants like she's clawing to see what's inside.

I look up to the ceiling as my chest tightens so much I can barely breathe.

Gina grabs for my cock and is shocked when she sees I'm completely limp. Looking up at me she frowns, "Mr. Ashley… I've never seen you like this. Let me see if I can help with this situation." She leans down and sticks my entire cock in her mouth, moving her tongue around.

I gasp as the feeling makes my chest burn and my stomach nauseous. I know I don't really want this no matter what I just saw Allison doing.

I jump up, pushing Gina off of me. "I'm sorry… I can't," and I run out of her house, jumping in my car and speeding away.

I pull over in Golden Gate Park to try to gain my composure and think about what I plan on doing now. Turning my phone back on, I see multiple text messages and voicemails from Allison along with one from a number I don't recognize.

I listen to that one first to see who it is:

"Charlie, um, it's Alex. Look, I deserved that. I don't know what came over me. I… I just wanted to let you know it was all me. Allison had nothing to do with it. I saw her crying and, shit man, I can't lie, I have feelings for her. But that's my problem. Please don't be mad at her. She made it very clear after you left that she wants nothing to do with me. So… I'm sorry."

I rub my eyes as I play the message again.

Fuck. God, what have I done? Thank God I left Gina's. But shit, I kissed her.

My stomach turns as I listen to Allison's messages next:

"Charlie, please baby. Where did you go? Please answer my call."

The next message:

"Charlie, I swear, I want nothing to do with Alex. He kissed me. I promise.

Please call me back."

The final message:

"I love you Charlie. I can't stand this feeling. Where are you?"

My eyes start to well as I fight back the tears wondering how I can face her again.

Here she wanted nothing to do with this man who took advantage of her and I go straight to a former client. How can I be such an idiot? She's going to hate me.

I need to clear my head so I drive to Twin Peaks, hoping the view and fresh air will calm me down. As I pull up I see Allison sitting on the wall, waiting for me to show up.

I park the car and slowly walk up to her with my head down, not sure how to approach her.

When I'm close I ask, "How did you know I would show up here?"

"Because I know you Charlie, all of you. I knew this was your place."

I reach out to hold her hand as I look down. "I got your messages." I look at her and see her eyes are red and swollen from crying which breaks my heart even more. "Alex called me, too."

"Please believe me Charlie. I don't want anything to do with him. I quit."

I hold my finger up to her lip, "Shhh, it's ok."

"Where have you been? I was worried sick."

I fall to my knees in front of her, willing to beg for her forgiveness. "I messed up Allison." I look at her, tears running down my face.

Allison gives me a sour look. "What are you talking about Charlie?"

"Please forgive me. I've never felt that feeling when I saw you with him. It felt like you drove stakes right through my heart. I was mad. I was scared. I had to do something or I felt like I was going to die."

"Charlie, you're scaring me. What did you do?"

"Then when I left I saw a billboard going up in Union Square. Allison, it's our photo, from our modeling shoot in Paris. Seeing you, us, together, I felt I had died all over again. Then I turned on the radio and *Savior* was playing."

"Yeah, Alex told me the photo was going up, but Charlie, tell me what you did."

"Please know that when I got there I couldn't do it and I left. Even though I still thought you kissed Alex, I couldn't go through with it."

"Charlie...?"

"Allison, I went to an old client's house. The one we saw at the Halloween Ball."

Allison pushes my hands off of her, "You did WHAT?"

"Allison please, please understand what was going through my head. I've never dated. I've never been in love. Seeing you with him was worse than any feeling I have ever felt." I grab her hands again, "Even the feeling when my parents passed away. I couldn't stand the idea of losing you or seeing you with another man. I lost my mind. I had to do something or I would have killed myself."

"Charlie, don't talk like that."

"It's true. Allison, I can't imagine my life without you. I just saw a glimpse and I can tell you it's something I never want to feel again. I'm sorry. I went to her house. I kissed her but that was it. I couldn't do anything else. She wanted to," I look down, embarrassed by my confession. "She tried but I knew it was not what I wanted. No matter what I just saw you doing. I walked out without doing anything else. I promise."

"Fuck Charlie! The first time anything goes bad between us you run right back into that lifestyle. How is that supposed to make me feel?"

"Allison please, I was so scared I had lost you. You left the house so upset with me then I saw you kissing Alex when I came to surprise you with flowers. What am I supposed to think? I told you, I've never been in a relationship. I panicked. Please believe me. I know I will never go back. I couldn't. No one will ever be you."

Allison steps away, turning her back to me. I want so bad to reach out to her, and try to make all of this better but I'm frozen where I stand. I stare, praying she believes me and can find it within herself to forgive me.

My heart pounds as the silence between us grows. I watch as she tilts her head up to the sky, taking a deep breath before turning to me with a sad look in her eyes.

"Charlie, I can imagine what you felt. I'm sure it's the same feeling I am feeling right now, listening to you, but I know it was worse for you since you witnessed it." She looks at me, "We need a reset. Go back to this morning. Look, I'm sorry I got mad this morning."

"No Allison, I'm sorry. I should have told you. I just didn't want to upset you."

"I know Charlie, neither of us really know how to deal with all of this. Shit, nobody would. It is not exactly a common thing to be dealing with. But we're getting there. And I can tell you one thing for sure. The past couple of hours, when I couldn't find you, were the worst moments of my life as well. We're both in this. Together."

I place my hands on either side of her face, "Allison, I love you with all of my heart."

"I love you, too."

We lean into each other, kissing softly, emotionally, before holding each other tightly.

"I'm so sorry, Allison."

"Me, too, Charlie. Please, I don't ever want to hear you say goodbye again."

"I promise, I never will."

Seventeen

Charlie

"Happy New Year you two!" Nichole yells as she greets Allison and I walking into Paul's apartment where all of our friends are gathered to ring in the New Year.

Sonia walks up to Allison giving her a big hug, "It's about time you guys showed up. Do you know I get to look at your sexy ass on the billboard everyday when I walk into work?" she teases.

"Oh jeez, thankfully it's not the front of me."

"Yeah, I'm the only model in this family," Nichole butts into their conversation. "It's a hot photo though. You both look like you're about to devour each other."

"Oh and we did a few minutes after that photo was taken," I say laughing as Paul gives me a high five.

"Ok you guys. Enough of that," Allison says embarrassed.

"So what's going on with you now? Any new job leads?" Sonia asks Allison.

"Actually, Alex felt bad about what happened and set me up with another photographer. I have an interview next week. Sounds pretty promising."

"Oh good. That was really nice of him to do that."

"Nice of him?" I snap back, "Guy's a prick. He's lucky I didn't kick his ass more."

Allison gives me a snide look and I smile, winking back as I drink the beer Paul handed me.

"So wait, isn't there other big news for tonight?" Sonia asks looking to us both.

I pull an envelope from my back pocket, holding it up, "Yup, I have it right here. But not until midnight."

Sonia looks to Allison, "What do you think it is?"

"I have no clue. There's a 50/50 chance it's a boy or a girl..." she says sarcastically.

"Oh, come on. Charlie, what do you think it is?"

"Well, if my dreams are true," I pause to grab Allison and pull her into me, "And so far they are, it's a boy." I kiss Allison and everyone around us leaves, teasing us about being too touchy feely with each other.

The doctor did an ultrasound on Jacquelyn yesterday and I had them put the pictures and the sex of the baby in an envelope for the two of us to open together at midnight as our way of turning a new leaf for the New Year and our upcoming life together.

The party is going well with Paul being his obnoxious self, all over Nichole, and everyone thoroughly having a great time. Midnight rolls around and we pour champagne anticipating the countdown. Everyone gathers around Paul's balcony to ring in the New Year with the most beautiful view in the City.

"Hey, listen up!" Paul yells. "I know that everyone saw my fine ass girlfriend here with me tonight," he grabs Nichole, pulling her in closer, "I know you all are jealous but feel free to stay as long as you want because I'm about to disappear with her and celebrate the new year in another way." He raises his eyebrows to her as he pulls her away.

We all laugh, shaking our heads since we're used to their antics but before they leave I yell out, "Hey, don't forget the group WOD tomorrow. You said you would go."

"We will. I finally convinced Nichole to go, too."

"You did?" Allison's shocked to hear.

"I know, I know. Don't remind me." Nichole replies. "Yes, I am going to try CrossFit tomorrow. But only this once."

Paul laughs, "Sure, just like you said you wouldn't date. Just like me, once you've tried it you'll be hooked."

Nichole shakes her head, pulling Paul into the bedroom as we all begin the countdown, "10-9-8-7-6-5-4-3-2-1-Happy New Year!" we all yell in unison.

I wrap my arms around Allison, kissing her as slowly and lovingly as I can before looking into her eyes, "Happy New Year, baby. You ready?"

"Yes, what are we having?"

I look up to her, surprised at her *we* comment. This is the first time she's referred to the baby this way. My eyes tear up as I lean down to kiss her again.

I open the envelope and pull out the pictures of the baby. The top picture shows the baby's head with a profile shot of the little head, eyes and nose.

I slowly walk to the couch, suddenly weak from the sight of the picture.

Allison sits next to me, looking at the photo then at me. "Wow, look at that. That's your baby Charlie."

I look at Allison, my eyes full of tears. "I know. It's... it's amazing. It's a real baby."

Allison laughs, "Yes Charlie, it's a real baby."

"I mean, wow, look." I show her the picture.

"Is it a little more real now?"

I sigh, "Yeah," as I stare at the photo.

"So, what is it?"

I take a deep breath, flipping to the next piece of paper. "It's a boy..."

Allison's face lights up. "It is?"

"Just like in my dreams. Allison, it's all coming true. I'm," I pause, "we're going to have a boy. I think we should name him Lyric."

Allison looks at Sonia who is sitting next to us watching. "Well Charlie, I've never told you this but as long as I can remember I have wanted to name my son Lyric."

Sonia pipes in, "It's true Charlie. When she told me about your dream and the baby's name I about had a heart attack. It was just another sign that you two are meant to be."

"Really?" I look at Allison, surprised.

"Really Charlie... You know my love of music and how I pay attention to the lyrics of songs. I saw a little boy named Lyric years ago and just fell in love with the name. I wanted to make sure it was a boy before I said anything to you."

"So it is true. All my dreams are coming true."

I wrap my arms around Allison as the vision of my last dream where Jacquelyn came to pick our son up pops in my head but I quickly dismiss it, trying not to ruin the excitement for my son, our son.

PAUL

At 10 am we all meet at our CrossFit box ready for the group New Years WOD.

"Seriously? Only crazy people would meet this early on New Years day to workout. I swear, this place is a cult." Nichole says holding her head with dark sunglasses trying to hide her hangover.

We all laugh, knowing what Nichole is saying is totally true but we don't care.

"I know. It's crazy. I tell everyone yes, I drank the Kool-Aid and now I'm addicted but you just wait. You'll be happy you came with us this morning," Allison tries to comfort her sister. "I'm not going to lie, this is going to kick your ass but you'll have fun doing it. I promise."

"Ok everyone. Gather around, let's get this thing going." Andy yells out to all the other CrossFitters. "Ok, I want you to break into two equal teams. While one team runs 400 meters, the other team will be doing 20 squats, one burpee and six mountain climbers. Hence, 2016…" he smiles. "Everyone gets a stack of cards to count on their own. Only once the entire team is back from running can the next team begin their run. As you run out place the cards you turned in the bucket either labeled team one or team two. We will do three rounds. The team with the most cards in the bucket, wins. Everyone got it?"

Nichole looks at me, "Ok, help. Show me what these moves are again?"

I drop to the ground, doing a pushup before bringing my knees back into my chest and jumping straight up, high into the air, "That's a burpee." Then I go to a plank position to show her mountain climbers by bringing my leg up one at a time to my elbow. "And those are mountain climbers. Each leg together counts as one so only count when you bring your right leg up." I pull her in close into me, "Don't worry doll. You got this. And everyone does it together so I'll be right by your side. Even on the run." I kiss her sweetly trying to encourage her more.

Nichole shakes her head, "Why did I agree to this?"

"Because you love me…" I reply.

Both Charlie and Allison look at Nichole to see her reaction before stepping away, giving us space.

Nichole sits still, not responding but not running either, which makes me smile. I don't need to hear her words though; her face says it all.

I smirk, leaning in, kissing her before I whisper, "I love you, too. And guess what? I got a text from my mom this morning saying she's in rehab. Hopefully just like you, she's coming around to the idea of change in her life, for the better." I grab her ass. "Did I thank you enough for going with me to see her?"

Nichole laughs, "Uh, yes, I was sore for a couple of days after that."

"Hmm… maybe we can do it again," I raise my eyebrows before ducking my head into her neck, kissing it before licking up to her ear.

Andy breaks our moment yelling out, "Ok, everyone ready?" He counts out the teams to make sure they're equal. "Ok. Three, two, one – Go!"

A big group piles out the door heading for their run. I hit Nichole's arm as we run next to each other, winking at her before giving her a sexy grin. "You got this baby. Don't over think it. Just roll with it."

She smiles back, "You know I'd rather be rolling around with you."

"That's my girl," I slap her ass as we finish the run.

As we enter the gym *Bad Girlfriend* by Theory of a Deadman plays over the speakers talking about her being naughty to the end and I can't help but smirk as I look at Nichole.

"Ok, team two – go! Team one start your squats," Andy yells out.

Nichole squats down and I can't help but reach out and grab her small round ass as she stands back up. "Oh Nic, that ass. I'm not sure I can make it through watching you dip down that low."

Nichole turns around, giving me a sexy grin, "Hands off, lover boy. Play your cards right and I see a hot shower in our near future."

"Ok you guys. Focus on the WOD," Allison laughs.

"I am. I can't wait to blow my wod," I can't help but respond in my cocky way.

After two rounds are complete we head out for the final run. I run up beside Nichole, sweat dripping down my bare chest. "How you doing doll?"

She gives me a don't-ask look making me laugh. "You got this. I've worked you out harder than this in my bed."

"True. I guess you'll owe me a long slow fuck after this, I'm not sure if I will be able to handle anything more."

I stop instantly, pulling her in close, both of us sweaty and breathing hard. "I can't wait to fuck you slowly. My dick got hard just hearing you say it." I push myself against her so she can feel me. "God, I will never get enough of you." I admit as I let her go and we head back in through the door to begin our squats.

This time Nichole turns around to face me as we both squat up and down. Staring at each other with nothing but hunger, trying hard to finish the WOD and not each other.

"Ok hurry up. The first group is coming back. Come on, push it. Finish strong," Andy yells out waiting for the last of the runners to return before yelling, "Time! Ok everyone. Put your cards in the bin."

I grab Nichole, holding her close, "You did it doll. See it wasn't that bad."

"Yay, Nichole. You did it," Allison yells out still trying to catch her breath.

"Good job Nic," Charlie holds up his hand to give her a high five.

"So, what did you think?" Allison asks.

Nichole smiles, "Ok, I'll admit it, that was fun. I don't know about drinking the Kool-aid or anything but yeah, I would come back."

"That's my girl. I love watching you sweat," I whisper in her ear.

"Gather around everyone, the cards have been tallied. Ok, group one had 167 cards and group two had 148… Group one wins. Good job everyone. Happy New Year."

Everyone cheers as Charlie celebrates with Allison before slapping high five to me. "Good job you guys. Happy New Year. I have a feeling it's going to be a great year," Charlie says.

Allison

Charlie and I spend the rest of the day being lazy, curled up on the couch both reading while wrapped up in each other's arms. Charlie looks from his book down to me lying on his chest. Looking back to his book, then me again, he puts the book down and reaches down to caress my breast.

I smile, moving my arm to allow his advance but continue my reading. Charlie takes full advantage and starts to caress me more, teasing me through my shirt before he unbuttons my top reaching in to feel my thin lace bra.

I'm trying to focus on my book but am having a hard time as Charlie pulls down my bra and rubs his fingers softly around my areola before pulling on my nipple. He teases it, pulling it hard then letting go and rubbing it again.

My breath picks up as I'm finally forced to put my book down, positioning my body for better access to Charlie's little game. I've never been so turned on by someone just playing with my breast and before long I'm panting, feeling just as aroused as I would be if he were licking my clit.

I wrap my leg around his, turning to my side, rubbing up against him, panting hard, feeling the need to cum growing deep inside. Charlie knows exactly what he's doing as he keeps up his game, pulling harder before letting go quickly and flicking my nipple back and forth.

My breath becomes deeper and harsher, the hunger inside me growing out of control.

Charlie moves quickly, pushing me to my back and wrapping his mouth around my nipple, licking slowly at first then quicker until he feels my body tense, ready to release.

Wrapping one hand in between my legs, he applies pressure on my mound as he bites my nipple softly, pushing me over the edge, letting go as he feels my body start to release in a beautiful orgasm while he sucks softly on my nipple.

I start to come down and am shocked that he just made me cum by just playing with my nipple.

"Wow. How did you do that? You never cease to amaze me. How do you know ways to make me cum that I didn't even know were possible?"

Charlie takes a short breath in, hiding his face in my stomach, ignoring my question and unbuttoning my pants.

I smile from my sexual bliss and knowing it's going to happen again shortly until the thought comes into my mind. *Shit, of course. That's why. This is what he did for a living. Ugh. Ok, don't go there.*

I push the idea out of my mind, and instead form a plan. His birthday is coming up and I finally have an idea of something special I can do for him.

Thinking positively again, I reach down, pulling Charlie up to my face to kiss him while I reach down to unbuckle his pants. Climbing on top of him, I slide down his hard body, kissing my way down to return the favor for my surprisingly phenomenal orgasm.

Eighteen

Dectective O'Brien

The last couple months have been crazy around the station. All kinds of fucked up shit has happened to really great people and my job has been more stressful than ever.

Seven months have passed since Jacquelyn Sanders was shot and since Jacquelyn is still alive it's not officially a homicide case so it hasn't been my top priority. I've tried to keep my tabs on it when I have time so things don't slip through the cracks but I still can't figure out who this girl is or why Jacquelyn kidnapped her.

I've gone back to the house to search the car more thoroughly for prints to find out who the girl is but found nothing. I even searched every chair in the dining room for a piece of hair or something that could track me to her but I've got nothing.

I just left Life Fitness where everyone says they met and I see they were telling the truth, all of them have memberships there. But I still have no clue why Jacquelyn drove all the way from San Rafael to go there. It was nothing special from what I could see. Just a normal gym that I'm sure there are plenty of in San Rafael.

I head back to my office and when I arrive I see there's a fax on my desk that I've been waiting for. Thankful it finally came through after all the red tape and months of waiting. I grab it, looking over the financial documents for Livingston, Inc., the company that Charlie works for. I couldn't find much information online about it so I had to dig deeper into their records.

It says they're a high-end firm offering consulting work for people who want to buy and sell real estate and that they're a subsidiary company of Deeper Holdings, Inc. I pause. *I know I just saw that name.*

Quickly, I shuffle through the paperwork on my desk looking for the warrant I had to get to check on the gym memberships. Once I find it, I hold it up reading, Life Fitness is a subsidiary company of Deeper Holdings, Inc. *Hmmmm… Ok, odd that Charlie works for the same company that owns the gym.*

Deeper Holdings, Inc. is a publicly traded company so digging into their records will be easier than it was for Livingston, Inc. I pull up the information online and there it is in front of me. The president and CEO of Deeper Holdings, Inc. is non-other than Kevin Hayes. *Diane's husband… I find it hard to believe this is all a coincidence… Finally, I am getting somewhere, just where?*

After doing more research but coming up with nothing I head home to have dinner with my wife.

"How was your day hun?" Sandy says as I walk through the door to a feast being prepared in my kitchen.

"Mmm, smells amazing in here. What are you cooking?"

"Leah's favorite, Lasagna. Poor girl is so swollen from this pregnancy so I told her and Nick to come over for dinner with the kids. They should be here any minute."

I hear the front door open and the sound of little feet hitting the floor as Andrew and Justin, my two grandsons, come running in the door screaming, "Grandma!"

They both run up to her leg, hugging her on either side, their faces light up from just seeing her.

She puts the spatula down and hugs them both at the same time. "There's my boys! I've missed you guys." She leans down to be closer to their size. "I got you guys something," she says with a playful smile across her face before grabbing both of their hands and running to the back room.

I smile seeing how good she is with them, with all of our kids and grandkids.

The next day I drive to the City, planning to sit in front of Charlie Ashley's place. My work load is finally lighter now so I'm try to look for things I might have missed in the Jacquelyn Sanders case.

I know something is up but I can't figure it out so I've decided to fall back on the old detective standby, a stake out. I'm hoping to learn something about Charlie that will tip off the case. And really, after the hell I've been through on other horrible cases, I'm happy to sit and relax for a while with nothing to do but watch.

First though, I head to Union Square to grab lunch. After parking I walk to the corner deli where I see a Guess Seductive Homme cologne ad that features Charlie.

Ok, so he's not lying about being a model. That's good to know.

But something catches my eye even more than him, the girl with him…

I walk back to my car to grab my briefcase where I've printed stills from the video surveillance.

Holding it up, I walk back to the billboard comparing the two. And yup, I was right, that has to be her. The photo on the billboard is of the side of her face, just like my stills and I'd put money on this being the same person.

Ok, now I'm getting somewhere.

I knew Charlie knew her but by the look of that photo I think they know each other very intimately. *But who is she?*

Then I wonder, if Jacquelyn is pregnant with his child, then obviously she wouldn't be happy about seeing this. I bet she found out they were sleeping together. Is that why she kidnapped this girl? Was he sleeping with both of them? Why? This girl is smokin'. Why would he even bother with Jacquelyn? She's nothing compared to her.

I walk away, confused still but feeling like I'm at least onto something now. After grabbing my lunch I drive to 1st Street, finding a place I can park and sit, watching Charlie's place for any sign of him.

After hours of waiting I'm about to give up when I see Charlie's Mustang pull out of the parking garage. He's stuck in stop-and-go traffic, so I'm able to get a good look at him as he approaches and I love seeing the fact that the girl I'm looking for is sitting in the front seat.

I snap a picture of her when she briefly looks my way. Both of them are smiling as she leans over kissing him softly on the lips before they drive away.

Ok, that was her and I would say they're definitely dating.

I check my camera; happy with the photo I got of her. It's finally a good picture that I can run face recognition software on.

Satisfied with my stake out, I head back to my office.

Once there I quickly load the photo into the face recognition software and search the Internet for a match for this girl. It doesn't take long for her Facebook page to pop up displaying pictures of her and Charlie.

I click on her page seeing her name for the first time, Allison Hayes.

Whoa, wait… She's Diane's daughter?

I look through all of her photos and there it is, one of her and Diane. Ok, this just got weirder.

I pick up the phone calling the gym to ask if Allison Hayes is a member. When I hear that she's not I'm even more confused.

Did Diane introduce Charlie to her daughter? Why? She had to though, how else would Charlie have met Allison if it wasn't through the gym? Is this really just a love triangle gone bad?

I don't buy that Charlie would legitimately be into Jacquelyn. He's a good-looking guy, a model for Christ sake. Is it the money? Are he and Allison in on this together? Did they plan this pregnancy for money and Jacquelyn caught on?

So many questions are running through my head and finally I think I have a motive.

I look at my watch and realize I have to go. Sandy has a doctor's appointment that she asked me to attend with her. I'm not really sure why. She's never asked me to go to this sort of thing but lately I'm trying to spend more time with her so I agreed. Even though I'm frustrated I have to leave when I'm finally getting somewhere, I grab my coat and head out the door.

Sandy and I walk into the doctor's office hand-in-hand waiting for the doctor. When we hear Sandy's name called she freezes, gripping my hand tighter before standing.

I get the feeling this is not a normal doctors visit and something is up. My stomach turns as we walk toward the doctor's office.

I can tell by the look on the doctor's face that it isn't good news. I look at Sandy before looking at the doctor as a huge knot grows firmly in my stomach.

"Ok Doc, give us the news. I get the feeling I'm the last to know what's going on here." I say, trying to get to the point.

Sandy grabs my hand, "Honey, please, sit down. I had some tests run last week and we're here for the results."

"Tests? What kind of tests?"

"I told you, I haven't been feeling good lately and I thought it was time I had it checked out."

I look at the doctor, "Ok, give it to us straight. I take it you found something."

"It's not good. I wish I had better news but yes, we did find something in her labs."

Sandy's hand starts to tremble and for the first time in our life together I'm noticing her breaking down.

"Sandy, I'm very sorry to say that you have stage four Melanoma."

My heart sinks to the ground. I have no air left in my body. I can feel Sandy's other arm reach to me but I'm numb and can't move.

The doctor continues, "I'm afraid Melanoma is the most serious type of skin cancer and your case is very advanced. That is why you are having these other symptoms. I'm so sorry to have to tell you this but your survival rate is not good."

I hear Sandy start to cry and I reach to hold her. This can't be happening.

Not to my Sandy. I'm going to retire and we planned on traveling the world. And the kids, they need her. I need her.

The doctor breaks the silence that has filled the air, "I highly suggest moving forward with an experimental treatment out at Stanford. It's expensive though and I'm not sure if your insurance will cover it."

I stand up frustrated, "What do you mean not sure if our insurance will cover it? Isn't that what insurance is for?"

"Well, yes and no. Unfortunately the survival rate with this is really not good and this treatment is showing hope for a few people but nothing is proven so insurance companies are denying it. They only look at the bottom dollar and in this case, it's just not proven enough to them to put the money out there."

"You have got to be kidding me? What other options do we have? How can they just let her die?"

"I know. It doesn't make sense but unfortunately that is the life we live in today."

"Ok, so let's just say they deny it. I'll pay for it. Take everything out of my retirement and savings. How much will it cost?"

The doctor shakes his head sadly, "In upwards of $825,000…"

"What? That's insane!"

"I'm so sorry. I wish I had better news or a way to help you. It's not looking good though. We can start a treatment here and start to work on your insurance but I'm sure they will just delay their decision giving you less treatment options just due to time remaining. I would suggest getting your affairs in order."

"No Doc, I can't lose her," I sit back down, holding her close as I start to tremble.

"It's ok, Sam." Sandy holds me tightly. She's stronger than me and seems to be accepting her diagnosis where I'm not, I will find a way to fix her. "I'm here now. Let's enjoy our time together and hope for the best. How much time do you think I have left Doctor?"

The doctor sighs, "Without further treatment, I'd say a year, if you're lucky. I'm sorry. I wish I had better news."

Sandy looks at me smiling, "We'll make it the best year yet. At least I'll get to meet my new granddaughter."

I wrap my arms around her as I start to sob on her shoulder. I'm officially broken. I can't stand the thought of losing her.

Nineteen

Allison

"Come on baby, you have to get up," I pull on Charlie's arm as he lies in bed.

"Allison, I love you but I told you, I don't do my birthday. You know why. Please, just let me hide for the day."

Charlie grabs the blankets, pulling them over his head to go back to sleep. Today marks 12 years since his parents passed. He hasn't celebrated his birthday since and says he spends every year hiding in bed.

I crawl in behind him, hugging him tightly. "But that was before me. I know today brings back a horrible memory for you but it also marks the day you were brought into this world by two people who loved you more than anything. And if they hadn't made you then I wouldn't have met you and my world would be crushed and I'd be all alone... Then the love bug came and got me." I sing the last portion trying to sound like Fergie's song *Clumsy*.

Charlie laughs, leaning over to kiss me sweetly. "She can't help it, the girl can't help it," he sings back.

"See! There's that smile I love. Come on baby. We're doing a birthday WOD in your honor today and you can't miss it. This year marks a new tradition, one with me in your life," I smile sweetly at him.

Charlie shakes his head, "You really need to stop looking so cute in the morning. You make it hard to say no."

"Great, get up, let's go. Paul and even Nichole are out front waiting for us."

Charlie gets out of bed with his shoulders slightly slumped over while trying to put on a happy face. The look in his eyes shows all the heartache for the last 12 years and I'm praying I can help change that for today.

We arrive at the CrossFit box and everyone walks up to tell him happy birthday. Looking around to see Paul and Nichole, along with his fellow Crossfitters makes Charlie's face show a small smile and he turns to kiss me. I know it's a small, un-said thank you and I hear it loud and clear.

This year marks his 29th birthday so the workout plays off the number 29. The WOD consists of two rounds of 20 box jumps, nine burpees, 200 meter run, then 20 thrusters, nine pull-ups, another 200 meter run, then 20 kettle bell swings, nine front squats and finish everything with a 29 calorie row.

"Damn Andy, couldn't take it easy on me could ya?" Charlie says laughing to Andy who has come over to greet him.

"Now why would I ever do a thing like that?" Andy laughs, "That would take all of the fun out of it. Happy birthday though."

Andy walks away and shortly after we hear *In Da Club* by 50 Cent play over the speakers, singing, "It's your birthday."

Charlie yells to Andy, "Really? Come on, you can do better than that."

Andy laughs, "Sorry man, I had to. Here, I know this is more up your alley."

My favorite guitar riff of all time plays loudly and I watch as Charlie lights up, giving Andy a nod of approval, saying, "This is more like it."

I've learned that the right song can bring him out of any funk and *Riot* by Three Days Grace seems to be his top choice, especially with this guitar intro.

Charlie looks to Nichole and Paul, "You guys ready for this?"

"Wait, this is way more than the New Years WOD I did. Charlie, you're lucky I love you because this is bullshit," Nichole yells out smacking Charlie on his arm.

Charlie laughs as Paul wraps his arms around Nichole giving her a small kiss for encouragement. "You got this doll. I'll be right here, watching over you."

"Giving me your *fuck me* look does not help me focus on the workout, Paul."

"But I'll reward you afterward to make your body nice and relaxed. That should give you something to look forward to," Paul says in his cocky way.

Nichole slaps his chest as we all start our warm-up together.

As we lie in bed, watching a movie I turn to Charlie, "Did you have a good birthday, baby?"

Charlie smiles fondly, "The best I've had in years just because you're here with me. Thank you." He kisses my lips sweetly for a second then smiles his sexy smile leaning in for more.

I laugh, "Hold on, I have one little present for you."

Charlie's lips form a straight line, "Baby, I told you, you didn't have to get me anything."

"I know. I didn't get you anything. I have a surprise for you. Do you trust me?"

Charlie tilts his head to the side, "Trust you? What do you have planned?"

I laugh but I know my shyness is showing through a little, "I asked you, do you trust me?"

"Of course I do baby."

"Ok, stay here. I'll be right back."

I walk into the kitchen, grabbing my iPod and scrolling to the playlist I made for his birthday consisting of my favorite Unwritten Law love songs. Once back in the room I head to the closet to grab the tie from my silk bathrobe and my black sleeping mask.

My hands start to sweat as my stomach turns with nerves knowing there is no turning back now. I've thought about doing this for a few weeks but going through with it, taking control, is another story.

Ok, just breathe. I can do this.

I take a deep breath walking toward him, hiding all my fears and giving him the sexiest smile I know how.

"What cha got there?" Charlie teases looking at the tie and eye mask.

"I know why you're so good at making love to me, it's something I should appreciate, rather than dwell on. But something came to me the other day. You always know exactly what to do, or say to make my body climb higher than anything I've ever thought possible because you take the time to really pay attention to me. So I thought, has anyone ever really paid attention to you? Have you ever had someone love on you the way you love on me?" I walk toward him swaying my hips and biting my lower lip.

Charlie's eyes grow wide, "Allison…"

"Yeah baby?"

"I, um…"

"It's ok. I'm in charge tonight."

I place the items on the bed as Charlie sits up on his knees on the end of the bed reaching to pull me close.

I grab Charlie's shirt by the hem and pull it over his head. Charlie leans to grab my shirt but I stop him, "Uh-uh, baby," I tilt my pointer finger back and forth at him, "I told you, I'm in charge."

I grab the eye mask, slipping it over his head, kissing him softly as I cover his eyes. Then grab my iPod, pushing play and placing the ear buds in his ears. Unwritten Law *Love Love Love* plays first and Charlie hums singing the chorus, "There will be love, love, love."

Now that Charlie can't see or hear, I try to bring his other senses to life. First by lighting a candle that fills the room with a fresh vanilla scent before walking back to him and picking up my silk robe tie. Being careful not to touch him, I wrap the tie around his back and lightly touch his skin moving it down from the back of his shoulders to around his waist before dropping it to the bed.

Taking my fingertips, I start at his shoulders lightly running my fingertips down his arms before grabbing his hands with each of mine and gently guiding them together. Holding them with one hand, I reach for the tie and slip it around his wrist, securing them together.

I watch as Charlie's mouth forms a slight smile making me giggle in response. I can tell he's enjoying this new form of submission, which is making me more willing to do everything I have planned.

I continue rubbing my hands along his body, leaning in to lightly kiss and lick his neck, his ear and finally his lips.

Elva is the next song on his play list and Charlie sways to the sound of the guitar strings. "But I'm all right, all right," he whispers in tune.

I lean up and surprise him by kissing him softly on his lips before he sings, "I'm in love with you in love with me."

I step back to remove my clothing, leaving Charlie waiting.

When I'm back, I run my hand over his cock, on top of his jeans and feel that he likes my little game so far.

Leaning down to my knees, I start to unbutton his pants, running my hand on the outside of his jeans before reaching in and freeing his enormous cock, teasingly licking up and down as I slide his pants further down to his knees.

Charlie tilts his head back, pushing his cock closer to my touch. I smile as I place his entire length in my mouth and suck all the way down to my throat, humming as I grab his ass, pulling him further into me. Pulling back, I lick my tongue around his shaft, swirling around before taking him back in.

Charlie's arms are tied in front of him so he puts his wrists behind my head like he's holding on for dear life.

I tease him for a few more minutes before wrapping my hands around his girth and stroking him up and down, twisting my hands with every stroke as I lick his tip making his sweet pre-cum slide out. The taste sends my desire through the roof as I speed up my strokes, motivated only to taste more of him.

Charlie's legs start to shake as he tenses up so I slow down taking him fully in my mouth, teasing him to lose control.

Once I know he can't take it anymore, I work my hands again, faster and faster until cum explodes out of him straight down my throat as he grunts his satisfaction.

I continue softly sucking until he's dry, twirling my tongue around, playing with his sensitive skin until I feel him relax and sigh with gratitude.

Taking him by surprise, I swiftly stand up and push him back on the bed so he falls with a big thud with his pants still wrapped around his legs.

After removing them I walk to get my bag from the living room. Inside of it I remove a feather, a small leather flogger and a smooth cold rock. Now that he's cum I want to bring his senses to the surface again through only my touch.

Charlie lies on the bed with a huge grin on his face as I hear another song playing *Because of You*. The song has a faster beat so Charlie moves a little, nodding his head to the music that's bringing him back to focus as he sings, "Because of you, ohhhhh, now, my dreams came true."

I can't help but laugh seeing him naked, tied up and singing with a sweet smile on his face.

I walk to the bed rubbing my hands up his legs before straddling him, sitting on his waist, untying his hands and repositioning them above his head before tying them to the headboard.

Holding the feather with my two fingers, I slowly run it down the side of his face, around his jaw and down his neck before swirling it around his nipple. Charlie smiles at the soft feeling so I lean down and lick his nipple. He literally moans from my touch and I feel life coming back into his cock underneath me.

Next I take the rock and run the same path on the other side. The feeling is different, cold, yet smooth and soft. After rubbing over his nipple I run the rock down his stomach, around his cock and rub it softly on his nut sack.

Another song begins playing *I Like the Way*. I pause when I hear him sing, "The only girl I loved, it'll be the last one. I know, I know."

I sigh, loving this man before me even more. Rubbing my thumb over his lips, he sticks his tongue out to lick my finger and I lean down, sucking his tongue into my mouth.

Next I grab the flogger and, without trying to move too much so he's surprised by my touch, I turn to run it over his legs, sliding it up one leg and down the other. The leather strands fall over his legs making it feel like a hundred things touching him at once.

I let the feeling engulf him before I swiftly take a swing, slapping his leg with a small thud. He jumps, surprised by my movement, then sooth him as I twirl the flogger over the spot I just hit.

Jumping off of him, I turn around and move down to his feet so I'm facing him before I repeat my little game, slapping him on the other side. This time after I do it, I bend down and lick the area, soothing it before licking over to his cock and sliding up it again, bringing him fully back to life.

I love how just the touch of my tongue fills his cock with a hardness that rocks my world. I'm dying to take him again in my mouth but hold off, knowing I need to keep with my little game as I move the flogger up his body, hitting him then licking and kissing the area back to life.

Charlie's face stiffens and for a second I hesitate, not sure if he's liking it or not, until I look down at his hard cock, standing straight up, as hard as I've ever seen him, literally pulsing with need.

Straddling him again, I lean down removing one of the earbuds, whispering in his ear, "You like that baby? Am I turning you on?"

Charlie just sighs, mumbling, "Um, hmmm."

I place the earbud back in his ear as yet another song begins playing *Rest of My Life.*

Charlie

With the song playing through my head and the feeling of Allison touching me in a way I've never felt before, I'm overcome with emotion, especially on this crazy emotional day. My heart starts to pound as I clench my eyes shut trying to fight back the tears. My lips quiver as I sing, "Say you won't leave for the rest of my life."

Allison slowly removes my mask and my earbuds, looking straight into my eyes whispering, "I'm yours forever. I love you, Charlie." Then leans down and kisses me, wrapping her hands around my face, leaning down and rubbing her body against mine.

My arms are still tied but I try to push my cock up to her, needing her to touch it, feel it, and thrust it inside her.

Slowly she reaches down, positioning herself on top of me and slides down my length before sitting as still as she can, driving me absolutely to the brink.

After a second she starts to sway her hips and move me back and forth inside her. She leans in for another kiss and the sensation of her lips makes me moan.

I hear her breathing pick up as she starts pressing harder and harder against me. I angle my hips up, thrusting harder into her as she slams down around me, throwing her head back in pleasure.

I'm dying to touch her but my hands are still tied above my head. I have to admit though, not being able to is actually turning me on even more and I'm having a hard time stopping myself from cumming too fast.

I clench my teeth, grinding into her more, needing to make sure she cums before I blow my load.

I feel her arms tighten as her body starts to shake making me thrust even more, filling her insides as I explode. Allison screams out and I know I'm hitting her at the right spot, sending her body into convulsions.

She collapses around me, barely able to breathe and so weak she can't hold herself up anymore. We lie together, trying to slow down our breathing.

She starts to untie my arms and rubs around my wrists, bringing blood flow back into them.

I don't care about my wrists, I'm dying to touch Allison, feel her soft skin with my fingers. I roll her around so I can be on top of her and kiss her deeply as I thank her for the best birthday I've ever had.

Twenty

Allison

Charlie's lying on the bed watching his favorite street racing show *Street Outlaws*. Tomorrow is the day, May 6th, and Jacquelyn is scheduled for a c-section so the reality of everything from the last nine months is about to come to head.

I'm so nervous for what is to come. Everything has been so good between Charlie and I and I don't want this time together to end. I like to think I'm strong enough to stay with Charlie if Jacquelyn does wake up but if I'm honest with myself, I just don't know.

I walk up and lie down next to him, wrapping my arms around his chest and laying my head on his shoulder. Almost immediately I feel tightness in my chest and that familiar pull in my stomach, amazed that just by touching him my desire grows from not even thought about to barely able to control myself.

I can't keep my hands off of him so I slowly start running my arm around his chest and down his pants, rubbing over the swishy lounge pants he has on. Charlie looks at me as the corners of his lips tilt up before going back to watching the show.

I know he won't mind so I continue my exploration of his body as my insides ache more and more.

I reach under his pants feeling that he feels the same and his length has tripled in size. Rubbing him softly I whisper, "Lift up, let me slide these down." Charlie's not one to argue my advances so he obliges and lets me do as I please.

Gathering wetness from my mouth, I sit up so I'm sitting beside him and gently start to stroke up and down his hard cock.

Charlie doesn't say a word, just smiles slightly while I caress him more.

Gathering more wetness, I work up and down his length enjoying how much touching him like this is turning me on even more.

I glance his way and my chest clenches at the sight of his face. I never get to see him while he's being pleasured and Goddamn he looks so freaking sexy right now. It's making me shamelessly want to take him right here and now.

After a long deep breath, I try to prolong my need just so I can look at his face longer. The crease between his eyebrows, the darkness in his eyes, all show the burn within him building. He slowly parts his lips, exhaling as he looks at me. We catch eyes making my body overheat and my breathing even more harsh.

"Baby, if you keep that up I'm going to make a mess on both of us," Charlie says through harsh breaths as he's trying to contain himself.

"I want to see you cum. I've never seen your face while you cum. It's the sexiest thing I've ever seen just watching you now. Show me more."

Charlie leans up, kissing me softly, whispering, "As you wish," then lays back down more focused on me now than his show.

I gather more wetness, rubbing him up and down while I rotate my hand in a circular motion. I slow down, methodically moving slowly over his tip and back down.

Charlie's breath grows stronger as the look on his face grows darker. His lips part as he closes his eyes, tilting his head back while he starts to sway his hips up and down with my motion.

I feel his body tense then look to his face showing his jaw clinched and his eyes closed tight as pure ecstasy rips through his body and he begins to cum all over my hands.

The moment has me raging with desire to feel him more, taste him. So I wrap my mouth around him, licking it all up, surprising even Charlie.

He grabs my head, holding me there as a little more comes out. "Oh my God, Allison... I think that was the hottest thing I've ever seen you do."

I pull back, a sexy grin on my face. "Yeah, you like that baby?"

"More than I could ever tell you. Thank you." He grabs his cock, squeezing it tightly as a little more cum comes out.

I lean down and slowly lick it up sighing at the wonderful taste of him.

Charlie tilts his head back in awe, only taken out of his euphoria at the sound of his text going off. He sighs and grabs it, leaning up to kiss me before looking at it.

Quickly he sits up. "What the fuck?" Charlie yells out in disbelief.

"Baby, what's wrong?" I lean up so I'm leaning over his back looking at his phone. Charlie shows me his phone where I read:

I know what you did and why you did it. You better hope she lives or be prepared to be meeting with me if you want to keep your little secret safe.

"What?" Who is that from?" I ask.

"I don't know. I don't recognize the number."

"What should we do?" My voice starts to crack with fear. "Who could it be?"

"I have no clue." He texts back:

Who is this? I don't know what you think you know but you're wrong because there is nothing to know.

I look at him, "Charlie, I don't like this. What could they be talking about?"

Charlie leans over to kiss my cheek. "Don't worry, baby. I'm sure it's nothing."

I hear it vibrate again and Charlie hides his phone so I don't see the response.

I look at him, eyeing his phone that he quickly put on the bed face down. "What was that? What did they text back?"

"Nothing. They didn't text back."

"Charlie, you're a horrible liar. Tell me. Remember, no more secrets. Not now. Not ever."

Charlie sighs, grabbing his phone, slipping it into his back pocket trying to be playful to distract me. "I'm hurt." He leans in, kissing my neck trying to push me down to the bed.

"Charlie, come on. I know they responded," I push his chest back to a seated position. "Tell me." I give him an I'm-not-playing look making Charlie sigh, looking down.

"Allison, I just don't want you to worry. Please, let me deal with whatever this is. It's my problem and I don't want you brought into this any more."

"Ok, now you're worrying me. Tell me what they said."

Charlie stands up. "I'm sorry. I won't. Please, drop it."

"Charlie! You said we wouldn't have any more secrets. You need to tell me."

"Allison, please. Just for this once. Let me deal with this. I don't want to worry you or get you involved."

"But I am involved. It's too late to not get me involved. Charlie, our entire lives are going to change tomorrow. Tomorrow! This all started with you keeping secrets from me so excuse me if I don't trust you," I start to yell, extremely pissed off all a sudden.

"Allison, no. Don't say that. You can trust me." Charlie grabs for my hands holding them in front of him as we stand inches apart.

I look down. "Charlie, I'm trying to be strong. But I feel like I can crack at any minute. I'm still not sure I can even do this. I don't need to think there is something else you're keeping from me. Don't push me away. Not now. Not if you want me to stay here. With you. With Lyric. I can't start out our life this way." By the end of my statement I'm barely whispering.

"Allison, baby. Look at me. Don't talk like this. Please don't tell me you're having second thoughts. I need you here with me. Lyric needs you." He pulls me in closer, so we're touching as he leans down and places his forehead against mine. "You're his mother."

I take a sharp breath in, "But what if his actual mother does wake up? What then? I'm step-mom...? Charlie, I..." I try to push myself away from him as my eyes fill with tears.

"No Allison, don't think like that. You say so yourself, 'everything happens for a reason.' We have to have faith. If she wakes up we will figure it out and everything will be ok."

"How can you say that? You don't know. Charlie, the woman threatened to kill me. Did you forget that little fact?" I yell as my tears turn to anger.

"Allie, no. I'm sorry. I didn't forget. I know you have been through a lot," he looks down ashamed. "All because of me. But Allison, please. Don't do this now. I need you, more now than ever. My son, our son, will be born tomorrow. I have to believe everything will be ok. We will be ok."

"If you honestly think that Charlie than why are you hiding your phone from me? Who texted you?"

"Allison, I don't know. I'm being honest. I have no idea who sent this text and why. I really just don't want to hurt you. If you really want to read it you can. I hope you would just listen to me and trust me. I'm not trying to hide something from you. I'm trying to protect you. I will tell you this. You don't want to know what this says. And I don't want you to know until I know who it came from and why."

I look up, shocked. Tears start to fall down my face as Charlie pulls me in closer. "I love you. Please, I don't want you to have all of these feelings, all of these doubts. Especially now, especially with what's happening tomorrow. This should be the best day of our lives. Our baby will be here." He looks down directly into my eyes, "You hear me. *Our* baby."

I look up, not being able to fight the tears that flow down my face freely. "Then tell me. I can handle whatever you have to tell me."

Charlie reaches to his back pocket and hands me the phone. "Please know. I'm giving you this because I love you. And I don't want you to read it because I love you. Decision is yours."

I look down to his phone. Holding it with both hands but I don't swipe it on. I look up at him, looking into his eyes then back to the phone. Slowly I throw it down on the bed. "Ok Charlie. I won't read it. But please don't keep me in the dark. If they text back you let me know. If you don't want me to know what it says I'll trust you. But if you're in trouble you let me know. No secrets. Ok?"

Charlie grabs me tightly, holding me close to him. "I promise. Thank you. I just don't want to worry you over something I don't even know is worth worrying about. Come on. Can we get back to what you started a few minutes ago? I do believe I owe you an orgasm now." He smiles his sexy smile, wrapping his hands around my neck and pulling me in for a kiss.

I'm too worked up to kiss him back. "I'm sorry. Give me a second." I turn and walk into the kitchen for water.

Charlie

Once Allison's gone from the room I fall down on the bed. I've been trying to keep my anxiety for tomorrow at ease but now, after the text and the fight with Allison, I'm truly and emotionally terrified. So terrified that I do something I swear I never would after my parents died. I pray.

Please, God. I've never asked you for anything. And I know I'm not religious, or anything, but if you are there. If you are listening. Please. Please make tomorrow ok. Can you please…

I pause, not sure how to finish my thought. How can I ask God to not let her live?

Just please make everything ok. I love Allison. Please give her strength to stay with me.

I pause again.

No matter what happens.

Twenty-One

Allison

I look down to my hand that is gripped around Charlie's. Neither one of us wanted to be in the delivery room so we're sitting silently in the waiting room waiting for news.

My stomach turns and my chest is so tight I can barely breathe. Charlie leans his head back against the wall behind him, closing his eyes taking a deep breath in and out. I'm assuming he feels the same way I do but I can't work up the never to ask.

"I wish my parents were here," Charlie whispers.

I'm shocked to hear Charlie's confession. He's never spoken of them besides relaying the dreams he had that they were in. I grip his hands tighter. "They are, baby. I know they are. Just like in your dreams. They're always with you. And they know their grandson is being born today. I really believe that."

Charlie opens his eyes and looks at me with his head still leaning back and takes a deep breath, then whispers, "Thank you. Thank you for being here with me. I know this is a lot for you. I don't know what I would do if you weren't here with me right now."

My heart aches for him. I love this man and he's been through so much. There is nowhere I would rather be than right by his side. A small tear runs down my face as I hear a familiar voice timidly say hello. I turn my head to see my mom and dad walk through the door.

We still aren't speaking but seeing her, after all this time and in this very tense, scary moment, I'm nothing but grateful to see them both standing there, especially my mom.

"Charlie… Allison… I hope it's ok that we are here," my mom says while holding my dad's hand and arm firmly for support.

"Mom!" I run up, wrapping my arms around her, giving her a huge hug as tears fall uncontrollably.

She instantly starts to cry, gripping me tightly. "Oh Allison. I'm so sorry. I miss you so much."

I don't want to think about anything. Right now I just really need my mom and having her there to support us means more to me than I ever thought possible.

Now I fully understand Charlie's comment about wanting his parents there. I didn't know how bad I needed my parents until the second they walked in.

I turn to Charlie then back to my parents, for the first time, fully understanding the pain he has been going through the last ten years.

I look my mom in the eyes then tilt my head to Charlie in an un-said motion that he needs a mom right now, too.

She loosens her grip on me and walks over to Charlie who stands as she approaches. "Charlie, I know I will never be like a mom to you but I'd like to try." She looks to me for reassurance. "At least I will be a Grandma in your life. If you guys will let me."

Charlie shakes his head *yes* as a tear falls down his face and he reaches over to give her a big hug. I know hearing he has the support of a family in his life now means more than anyone could ever know. I can't help but let the tears flow down my cheeks.

She whispers, "I'm so sorry Charlie. This is all my fault."

Charlie stops her and pulls back looking into her eyes. "This is nobody's fault. This is my son." He looks at me, holding out his hand to grip mine again. "Our son. I will never look at this as anything but a blessing."

My dad walks up, placing his hand on Charlie's back. "You make me proud to say you're a part of our family."

They smile at each other for a moment as a nurse walks in, "Excuse me. Which one of you is Charles Ashley?"

We all freeze, looking at the nurse before Charlie grabs my hand tightly, stepping forward saying, "I am."

She smiles halfheartedly, "Can you please follow me? The doctor would like to speak to you."

He looks at me, pulling on my hand with an *it's time* look on his face.

I can't move. I'm completely stuck. It's like my feet have been glued to the ground and my legs forgot what walking even feels like.

I get lightheaded, my brain swimming with possibilities. These last nine months, not knowing what will happen, will she live, will she die? And the baby. Lyric. Everything is coming down to this moment. Right here. I think

I'm going to be sick. If I can't move even a centimeter forward, how can I move a lifetime forward?

My dad wraps his arm around me. "It's ok Allison. We'll be right here. Go with him."

I look up at him, still not able to move or breathe. Charlie steps closer, wrapping his arms around my waist, pulling me in so we're centimeters apart and whispers, "Breathe," before kissing me softly.

He steps away holding my hand tightly and pauses when he sees I'm not following him. He looks back with pain in his eyes. *Please Allison.* He mouths to me. *Please come with me.*

I take a deep breath in then slowly start to move forward looking straight into his eyes. I need those eyes looking back at me. They are my comfort, my everything. As long as I have those to look into I know I can do this. My whole body trembles with fear as I wrap my other arm around his arm, holding myself up as we walk out the door. I've never felt so faint in my life but having my rock, my Charlie, by my side helps calm me more than ever before.

I can do this.

We enter a room where a doctor has his back facing us writing in a chart. He turns when we enter and it's hard to read his facial expression.

Not able to wait a second longer, Charlie asks, "So what happened? Is my son ok?"

The doctor looks at him, then at me. "I'm sorry to say but Jacquelyn didn't make it."

Charlie looks at me, trying to hide his happiness, knowing this is not something people would normally be celebrating, but oh my God I feel like I could float away on could nine right now. My chest opens up, I can finally breathe. Filling my lungs with what feels like the best air ever created on this earth. I try really hard not to smile and just grip Charlie tighter.

The doctor continues, "Once we started the procedure her blood pressure started to spike and we tried everything. We were hoping the hormones released after the baby was delivered would bring something back to life but the medication we had to give her had the opposite affect and it was too much for her body to handle. It turned into an emergency surgery to get the baby out as fast as we could so we could try to revive her but unfortunately there was nothing we could do. She was already gone."

We both look at each other, knowing what our hearts are feeling before Charlie looks back to the doctor. "And the baby?"

His frown turns slightly up, "Congratulations. It's a boy. He's this way." The doctor puts his hand on Charlie's back, "Come meet your son."

Tears instantly flow down Charlie's face and I can only think they are tears of happiness, tears of relief, tears of sorrow for his parents, and tears of joy for his son. He wraps his arm around my waist and leans in to give me a sweet kiss before pulling back and whispering, "Come on. Let's go meet our son."

We walk into another room to see a little boy wrapped up in a blanket in a clear bassinet with a nurse standing over him.

She looks up to Charlie and smiles, "This must be your beautiful little boy." She looks down, then back at him. "He has your eyes."

Charlie's eyes well up again as he leans down to see his son for the first time. He looks at me, then to the nurse. "Can I hold him?"

The nurse laughs, "He's yours sweetie. You can do whatever you want with him."

Charlie's face lights up as he reaches down and timidly wraps his arms around his son and begins to lift him up to his chest. He cradles him in his arms looking to him as he rubs his soft head that is lightly covered with soft brown hair.

My heart melts like never before. Seeing a brand new baby is a feeling that can't even be described. I was there the moment Sonia's daughter was born and this feels the same. That instant love, the instant happiness and knowing you would do anything for that baby is all too consuming.

You want to hold them tight but you're terrified to hurt them because they are so tiny. You can't help but stare at them as your heart grows five times bigger than you ever thought possible.

I know, in this moment, that I can love Lyric as my own son. He is mine. I am his mom. Just like I love Sonia's daughter as my own. It doesn't matter if I didn't give birth to him; we are a family now.

I'm his mommy.

He looks at me as more tears fall. I step toward him, leaning down and kissing Lyric's head before leaning in and kissing Charlie on the lips as tears fall from my eyes as well.

"He's beautiful, Charlie," I whisper looking back up at him. "Hello Lyric," I pause, looking up to Charlie and then down to Lyric again. "I'm your Mommy," I say closely to him before kissing his head.

Charlie's body visibly constricts as he lets out a sob he can't hold in, wrapping his arm around me so the three of us are in our first family hug. Hands down this is the best moment of my life. One I will remember forever. The birth of our son. I hold on to Charlie and Lyric never wanting to let go.

We sit in an embrace until there's a knock on the door. Nichole walks in whispering, "Can we come in?"

We both look up, wiping our eyes, smiling as Nichole, Paul, along with my mom and dad all walk through the door.

Nichole squeals as she jumps over to where we're standing smiling from ear to ear, "Let me see him, let me see him!"

She wraps her arms around both Charlie and I looking down to Lyric. "He's beautiful. God Charlie, he looks just like you."

Charlie looks at her then back down to Lyric, rubbing his head again, "He does, doesn't he?"

Paul walks over placing his hand on Charlie's shoulder. "Congratulations, bro."

"Thanks man. I'm glad you're here."

I look at Charlie, "Can I hold him?"

"Of course," Charlie hands him over to me and steps back, taking in everything that his life has become.

A huge smile grows over his face. We catch eyes as we both smile and whisper, "I love you," at the same time.

I look over to my parents who are standing next to the door, timid about their presence. I look back to Charlie who shrugs and nods his head their way.

I'm ready to forget everything that's happened. I can forgive my mom because I know now that no matter what, family is the most important thing. We need them in our lives. Lyric needs them. We will show this little boy that he is more loved than anything in the entire world.

Slowly, I walk toward them with Lyric in my hands and smile, "Lyric. I'd like for you to meet your Grandma and Grandpa."

My mom covers her mouth with her hands as tears flow freely down her face. She places her hand on his head softly and smiles at me mouthing the word, *Thank you.*

I whisper back, "You're welcome. Here, would you like to hold him?"

She reaches out, without hesitation, and wraps her arms around her new grandson. My dad leans down and kisses my mom on the head before lightly running his hands over Lyric's head. "He's beautiful you two."

Charlie walks up behind me, grabbing my shoulders and lightly kissing the back of my head. "He really is."

I lean back into Charlie, placing my hand on his while resting the back of my head on his chest and let out a breath I feel like I've been holding for the last nine months, knowing now that my life is complete.

Twenty-Two

Charlie

The three of us spent the night in the hospital before bringing Lyric home for the first time. Since Jacquelyn could not verify that I was the father, the hospital ran a paternity test and when it came back that Lyric was definitely mine we were allowed to take him home.

Allison and I hold hands as Lyric sits quietly in his car seat in the backseat of the Mustang. With smiles covering both of our faces, we head toward our future together.

Marry Me by Train comes over the radio and I can't take my eyes off of Allison as we sit at a red light.

I lean over kissing Allison on the cheek, whispering, "Getting the nerve to say hello in the café was the best thing I ever did."

Adjusting to having a baby took a few days but we're working through it with nothing but love for one another and love for Lyric. Our life was complete until the third day when my text went off again:

I see she died. Lucky bastard. Lucky for me too.

I'm thankful that Allison is not in the room as I grit my teeth replying back:

Who is this? Why are you texting me?

*You'll see soon enough. I know you did this for her money and
I want some too or I'll turn you in.*

What are you talking about? What money?

Don't lie to me. You know what money.

NO I DON'T!!!

Pretend all you want. I'll get mine. Just you wait.

**Look, I don't know who you are or what you think you know
but you're wrong. Leave my family alone!**

I slip my phone in my back pocket just as Allison walks in from the
bedroom holding Lyric and thankfully not noticing anything that was going
on.

"I'm going to put this little angel down for bed, do you need anything
from in here before I do?" she says.

I walk over, kiss Lyric on the head before leaning in and kissing Allison
on the lips, "No, I'm good. Night buddy," I whisper to Lyric.

Once I walk out of the room I grab my cell phone from my back pocket
to see that there's a reply:

*Meet me in an hour at the front entrance of Pier 39. I'll find
you.*

My jaw clenches and my eyes squint, reading the text again. *Shit. What do
I tell Allison? I can't tell her where I'm going.*

She walks back into the living room and sits down on the couch sighing,
and exhausted from the last few days.

I think up a plan. "Hey baby, Paul's heading to the gym, do you mind if I
go get a WOD in?"

Allison looks at me surprised, "You're not exhausted?"

I laugh, "Yeah, but I think it will do me good. Do you mind?"

"No, not at all. I'm probably going to put on a movie and crash right here.
Good idea to get a TV for out here so I can zone out," she laughs. "Since you
aren't tired you can get up tonight with him so I can sleep."

I laugh, "You got a deal. Love you, baby."

"Love you, too. Have fun. Tell everyone hello for me."

"I will." I lean in, giving her a long kiss before heading out the door. Once in the elevator I go up to Paul's place hoping Nichole isn't there.

As the doors to his apartment open Nichole walks by laughing, "Are you escaping already?"

Shit. "Um, no. Where's Paul?"

"Right here. What's up bro?"

"Can you talk?" I look from Paul to Nichole then back to Paul.

"Whoa. What's that look all about? Look Charlie. Allison's my sister. What's going on?" Nichole spits out, not holding anything back.

"Nichole please, I don't want you or Allison involved."

"Involved in *what*?"

Paul grabs Nichole's arm, "Please doll, can you give us a minute?"

"Look Charlie. If you hurt my sister I will kill you. She has given up so much for you! She's raising your child for Christ sake!"

"Nichole, I know. Please. It's nothing like that. I am trying to protect her."

"Protect her? From what? Tell me what you need to talk to Paul about. I'll decide if she needs protecting."

"Fine, have it your way. But please, don't say anything until I get back. Allison thinks Paul and I are going to the gym."

"Why are you lying to her? What's going on Charlie? Where are you going?"

I look at Paul, "Look man. I don't want to bring you into this because I don't even know what it is but I would feel better if I knew someone was there to at least look out for me. I don't want you near me but I want to know that if something does happen then someone will know. Does that make sense?"

"No Charlie, it doesn't. What's going on?" Paul replies.

I pull out my phone and show them the text messages. They both read them then look back up at me.

"What the fuck?" Paul questions.

"I don't know. I have to go find out why I'm getting these texts. They want to meet in a very public place so I'm comfortable with that. I just want someone watching out for me just in case."

Paul nods, "I got you. Let's go."

Nichole places her hands on both of us. "Whoa, wait a minute. You guys have no idea who this person is or what they want. You should call the cops."

"And say what Nichole? I used to be a male prostitute and I got my client pregnant, oh yeah, the one that you haven't solved the case for her murder and now some crazy is texting me saying shit I have no idea what he's talking about," I say, frustrated.

Nichole backs down, "Charlie, it's just, what about Allison? What about Lyric? This isn't safe."

I run my hands through my hair. "I know. But the text mentioned her and I need to figure this out before whoever this is does something more than text. What if they try to harm Allison or Lyric? I can't put them in any kind of risk. I'll go and figure out what they want and how much they know."

Paul turns toward Nichole, "It's ok. Pier 39 is a very public place. They won't do anything stupid. No one is that dumb. We'll be back. Why don't you go down and hang out with Allison?"

"Oh and act like nothing's going on? She would read my face like a book."

"Ok, yeah, you're right. Then stay here," Paul shrugs.

"No, if you go, I go. If you're just the lookout then you'll want someone with you anyway so you don't stand out. I'll let you rub my ass like a horny teenager while you spy," she teases.

Paul shrugs looking at me, "Sounds like a hell of a plan to me," he laughs.

"Fine you guys. Just stay back. But keep an eye on me, not just her ass."

"But have you seen her ass?" He hits my back joking around. "No worries man, we got you. Let's go figure out what the hell is going on."

It's dark at Pier 39 but there is still a good amount of people around. I sit on a bench at the entrance patiently waiting for someone to approach me. Paul and Nichole find an area for Paul to lean against so he's facing me. Nichole leans up against him, facing him as they embrace each other while waiting.

Not long after I sit down a man wearing a low baseball cap approaches me, sitting on the opposite side of the bench. He doesn't look my way but starts talking. "Continue to look forward. Don't look at me. Ok?"

I sit up straight when I hear the man talking to me. I look Paul dead in the eyes but don't look toward the man. "Ok."

"I know you and your little girlfriend scammed Jacquelyn for her money."

"Look, I don't know who you are but you're wrong. There is no money."

"Don't lie to me. I know you got her pregnant on purpose so you could get child support from her."

I gasp, shocked at what I'm hearing. "Are you kidding me? You think I did that on purpose? Look man. You have it all wrong."

"Don't lie to me. There is no way you legitimately were interested in Jacquelyn. Not when you have a little hottie like Allison."

I swiftly turn toward him, "You leave her out of this!"

The man quickly looks away. "I told you to face forward. Don't you dare turn toward me or I will involve her, you hear me?"

I turn to look forward again, taking a deep breath, trying to calm down. "Look, I met them at the exact same time. Believe me. Whatever you think you know you don't. Allison and I definitely did not plan this. If anything, Jacquelyn planned this."

"Oh yeah. Then why did she kidnap Allison?"

My breath is completely caught, "How do you know that?"

"I told you. I know everything. She found out about your little plan didn't she? So she tried to turn the tables on the two of you. Didn't she?"

"Look Mister. You're wrong. That is not what happened. And there is no money."

"Yes there is. I know there is. I want $825,000 or I go to the cops with your little scheme."

"$825,000! You're crazy! I don't have anywhere near that. Who the hell do you think I am?"

"You're the man that just inherited Jacquelyn's entire estate. Don't try and deny it. I'm *only* asking for $825,000. That's chump change for what you're worth now." The man's voice cracks when he says only and I get the sense there is something more happening here.

"No, actually, I didn't. Sorry. Again, I don't know what you think you know but you're wrong."

"But she has no family. And Lyric is her son so it all goes to him…" his voice growing desperate now and I'm actually starting to feel sorry for the guy.

"Nope, sorry to break it to you but you're wrong. I have no idea what's happening to her estate. It's not my problem. Lyric is my son and we have nothing to do with her."

The man is quickly losing hope. I can tell he's trying to be strong but he slips out, "But my wife."

The tension I felt from the man earlier has disappeared so I slowly turn my head to try to get a look at him. "Detective O'Brien?" I say completely shocked to see who's sitting beside me.

"Shit, no. Don't look at me. This conversation never happened." He swiftly stands up trying to walk away.

I grab his arm tightly to stop him. "What the fuck? What's going on?"

Detective O'Brien slumps his shoulders forward, defeated as he sits back down placing his head in his hands. "Look. I don't want to be here right now. This is not who I am. I just, I thought…" He looks at me, face to face for the first time and sighs. "Now I really fucked up. This is why I was always made to catch bad guys not be one."

I tilt my head at him, confused.

"It's my wife. She has Melanoma. Our insurance is denying her treatment and this was my last ditch hope. Dammit!" He slaps his hands on his knees in anger.

I place my hand on Detective O'Brien's back. "Look, I get it. I would do anything for Allison, too. But no, believe me, we absolutely did not plan this pregnancy to try to get money out of Jacquelyn. And no, we aren't getting any money from her estate," I pause. "I actually have no idea what's happening to her estate."

"Then what? Why did Jacquelyn do what she did?"

I pause again, looking into Detective O'Brien's eyes, not sure what he does actually know but I still play dumb, "I don't know what you're talking about?"

"I saw the tapes. I saw her tie Allison up. I saw Diane, who's Allison's mom, come in after you did. I saw you knee Jacquelyn and I saw the gun go off when you tried to get it away from her. I know you all belong to the same gym. The gym that is owned by the same parent company you work for. But nothing else adds up. So why?"

I sit back in my seat and sigh, "Well… I guess you'll never know. But you do know that none of us meant to harm Jacquelyn so there really isn't a case then. Just an unsolved break-in gone bad. And if you drop it then I'll pretend this conversation never happened. Deal."

Detective O'Brien sighs loudly, "Deal." He looks at me, "Look, sorry man. I just… my wife…"

I pat his back, "No worries. I wish I could help. I'd do the same for Allison."

I get up to walk toward Paul and Nichole when a man walks up quickly stopping me in my path.

"What the fuck is going on here? Why are you letting him go? He killed my wife!" the man yells at Detective O'Brien.

I hold out my hands to the man, "Hey, I don't know what you're talking about. I didn't kill anyone."

"Yes, you did. I saw the tapes. The same ones he did. Why are you letting him walk away?"

Detective O'Brien stands up quickly to approach the man. "Jack? What are you doing here?"

"What am I doing here?" he returns his question. "What am I doing here? I'm standing up for what is right. Standing up for my wife, Jacquelyn. This bastard killed her and is now going to steal all of MY money."

"You're Jacquelyn's husband?" I ask, shocked.

"Ex-husband," Detective O'Brien clarifies.

"I was her husband until this asshole came along." He looks at me, reaching behind him and producing a gun that he points directly at me. "This is all your fault. You set this up. You seduced her to take her money. You pushed me out. I put up with her shit for years, that money is mine. I earned it!"

My heart is beating out of control. Images of Lyric flash in front of me. No way am I leaving this earth. I have a son who needs me. I have to stay calm.

This man is obviously as crazy as Jacquelyn was.

I look up and Paul and I catch eyes. He's standing directly behind the man so I don't think he sees the gun but he knows something's up. I watch as he places his hands on Nichole, slowly moving her to the side, preparing for whatever he needs to do.

"Whoa, let's hold on here, Jack. Put down the gun. Charlie didn't kill Jacquelyn."

Jack points the gun at Detective O'Brien who instantly puts his hands in the air. I look at Paul who now has full vision of the gun. Slowly he moves Nichole completely out of the way. I watch as he says something to her and then very carefully starts to make his way toward us.

"He did kill her! I *saw* the videos. I had to know for myself what happened. I looked this asshole up months ago when I found out he was the supposed father. He didn't love Jacquelyn. He has that sweet little piece of ass he's always with."

"Hey, you keep her out of this!" I jump in.

He points the gun back to me. "You guys were in this together. You knew she was crazy but filthy rich. You knew you would get all of her money. Don't lie to me. But guess what? It's not going to happen. That money is mine and I'll do whatever it takes to get it back. And I came to do just that tonight but watched as you drove out of your place so I followed you here, only to find you meeting with him! Are you in on this, too? But wait, where are the other two people that were in your car?"

He looks around and sees Paul approaching from behind him. Turning around he points the gun at Paul. "Back up! You aren't part of this mess. Don't make me kill you, too."

"Hey, let's all calm down," Detective O'Brien says.

"Calm down! Excuse me?" Jack yells, moving the gun back to Detective O'Brien. "Why aren't you arresting him? Why are you meeting here instead of the police station? You saw those tapes months ago. Am I the only one who thinks that someone needs to go down for Jacquelyn's murder?"

"Jack, if you truly saw the tapes you saw that Charlie didn't shoot her intentionally," Detective O'Brien interjects.

"But he was involved. There was obviously something going on. He's responsible and I'm going to make it right. Jacquelyn deserves at least that!"

Jack raises the gun up to eye level, pointing it directly at me. "I will make it right," he says as he pulls the trigger.

My entire life flashes before my eyes. My parents. Growing up in Vacaville. Everything I've been through to be where I am now. Allison. Lyric. My entire world.

I hear screams as I hit the floor, hard. I can't see anything. All I hear is a man yelling, and a girl screaming but everything's black.

It takes me a second to come to when I feel someone moving over me. I realize that Paul landed on top of me, covering my entire upper half with his own.

"Fuck me!" I hear Paul yell as he sits up and my eyes adjust to the scene around me.

I hit my head pretty hard when Paul tackled me to the ground but other than that, I'm not hit. I sit up, turning to Paul who's gripping his arm. Nichole is wrapped around him, screaming at the top of her lungs for someone to call 911.

I turn to my left to see Detective O'Brien kneeling on top of Jack, with his hands handcuffed behind his back, talking on his phone.

Shaking my head once more I try to get up but am still a little dazed. On the second attempt I reach out to Paul.

"You ok man?"

Paul looks at his arm that's covered in blood, sighing he looks up to the sky saying a silent *thank you,* then looks at me, "Yeah, I think it just nicked my arm."

He looks at Nichole who is wrapped around him, hugging him as tears spill down her face.

She pulls back from him saying, "What the fuck Paul! You could have been killed!"

"Hey, better me than him. Charlie is my boy. I'd do anything for him. And Lyric needs him. I was raised without a father. There was no way I was going to let that happen to Lyric."

I stand up, walking closer to Paul and kneeling down. "You saved my life."

He looks up at me with a small smile, "Don't get all sappy on me bro."

I reach out to pat his back, "Thanks man. I owe you everything."

"Yeah, yeah, yeah, don't mention it. Just get me to a doctor before I bleed all over my clothes here." He's trying to joke but I can't help it.

I reach out, giving him a manly hug, "Thank you."

"You're welcome," he says returning my one arm hug.

I look up and see sirens approaching us. "Come on, let's get you up. Help is here."

I glance at Detective O'Brien who is walking Jack to the back of a waiting cop car. I nod and with a small smile he nods back.

Thankfully the bullet just grazed Paul's arm so he needed nothing more than a bandage to stop the bleeding. Paul and Nichole are sitting at the back of the ambulance with Nichole wrapped up in Paul's arms. I pull out my phone to call Allison to fill her in about everything that just happened. As the phone rings, I turn my attention to Paul and Nichole and watch their interaction. I watch as Nichole says, "I love you," to Paul and they kiss in a moment they feel that no one else is witnessing.

I can't help but smile. Knowing that feeling and so happy that Paul has found that love as well.

Twenty-Three

Allison

"Charlie, I know it's Unwritten Law and I normally wouldn't miss them for the world but do you really think we should go? I mean, Lyric is only three weeks old and we are heading to Vacaville in a couple of days for this Fiesta Days thing you keep talking about."

"Allison," Charlie grabs my hand pulling me in close. "There is no way we're missing this show. This is where we started. I'm forever in debt to this band. Without them, I would have never met you."

I smile, "Ok, if you put it that way," I tease.

"Besides, you know your mom is dying to watch Lyric for us. She'll be here any minute."

"Ok, give me a minute, I'll go get dressed."

"Hey," he grabs my arm turning me around and pulling me in close. "Will you wear the same outfit? The black Unwritten Law tank top with the red heart?"

I laugh, "Wouldn't dream of anything else," as I lean up to kiss him sweetly.

Paul, Nichole and Sonia meet at our place before we head out to Slims for the Unwritten Law concert.

Grabbing a drink at the bar, we all toast to Lyric and how grateful we are that everything turned out ok.

The lights go dim as the band takes the stage. Charlie and I engulf ourselves in their music as we dance and sing every song at the top of our lungs, enjoying being there with each other.

Charlie turns to me, talking in my ear so I can hear him over the band, "I'll be right back. Just heading to the bathroom real quick."

I smile and nod then go back to singing *Starships and Apocalypse.*

When the song finishes the lights go dim and Scott, the lead singer, walks to the microphone as a single light points down on him. "What's up San Francisco?" The crowd yells in response. "Ok, ok, thank you, thank you... we have a special surprise tonight." The crowd yells again even louder. "Sorry mother fuckers, it's not for you. It's for a special someone, a special girl in the crowd." The girls in the crowd scream wildly as Scott smiles a sexy smile turning to the dark corner off the stage.

An acoustic guitar starts to play the intro to *Rest of My Life* as Charlie walks out on stage playing the guitar. My eyes go huge as he meets Scott in the middle of the stage as Scott begins to sing.

I gasp as I stare in awe at him on the stage, covering my mouth as tears well up in my eyes. Sonia joins me on my left and Nichole on my right. I look to both of them as they smile from ear to ear. "How did he...?" I say, looking to both of them.

They laugh; pushing me through the crowd so we're next to the stage.

I watch as Charlie picks at the strings of his guitar, looking straight down to me as Scott sings about not wanting his girl to leave for the rest of his life.

Emotions flow through me as tears slowly work their way down my cheek. I can't take my eyes off the man I love, singing one of my favorite songs next to my favorite band. I almost want to pinch myself this moment feels so unreal. My heart is pounding so hard and my hands are starting to shake.

Nichole wraps her arm around me, pulling me in, kissing my cheek. I look at her and am shocked to see her eyes filled with tears as well.

Charlie plays the end of the song in the same acoustic guitar riff that started it while looking directly into my eyes. The crowd yells as Charlie looks at Scott who nods to Charlie, backing up so Charlie is center stage.

He removes the guitar from around his shoulder and hands it to Scott mouthing, *Thanks man,* before grabbing a box from his back pocket.

My heart sinks to the ground as I see the light teal box that he's pulled out from his pocket. He looks at me and slowly gets down on one knee. I feel my legs go limp and Nicole and Sonia grab my arms, steadying me to my feet as Charlie opens the box revealing a stunning carat diamond surrounded by a ton of little diamonds bringing out an antique look.

I grab my mouth as tears fall down my face. The crowd is so loud I can't hear him but see him mouth, *"Will you marry me?"*

I slowly lower my hands, revealing my huge smile as I shake my head *yes* with tears rolling down my face.

Charlie jumps off the stage and picks me up, swinging me around before kissing me with so much love and intensity I forget everyone around us. He holds me tightly to him, resting our foreheads together asking, "How did I get so lucky to find you?"

"I was sent to you. I'm your savior, remember?"

Charlie laughs before kissing me again like he never wants to let me go. I've never been so happy and I feel like I never want to let him go either.

Charlie

Allison's laying in bed staring at her hand with her engagement ring wrapped around her little finger. Life couldn't get any better. I come back to bed after making sure Lyric was back asleep and wrap my arms around Allison, pulling her into me.

"Good morning future Mrs. Ashley."

Allison smiles brightly gabbing my arm and pulling me tighter against her chest. "Good morning my future husband."

"God that sounds good coming from your lips. Say it again."

She smiles turning around so she is face to face with me and placing her hand on my cheek, "My future husband," emphasizing the word *my*.

I lean in, kissing her softly as my phone rings. "Ugh, don't people know we have a newborn," I grunt. "What time is it anyway?"

Allison laughs, "It's actually 9:15, you slept right through his five o'clock feeding."

I pout my lips, "Sorry baby."

"No worries. Who's calling?"

I look down, not recognizing the number, "Don't know." I answer, "Hello?"

"Hello. Is this Charles Ashley?"

"Yeah, this is him. How can I help you?" I sit up in bed so I'm holding the phone better against my ear.

"My name is Laura Stone. I am Jacquelyn Sanders' attorney."

"Yes…"

"Mr. Ashley, I was hoping you would have time to come into my office today. I have some things I need to discuss in regard to your son, Lyric."

"Whoa, why? He's my son. We did the paternity test. Why do I need to come in?"

"I'm sorry Mr. Ashley, I didn't mean to cause you concern. It's nothing bad. I have something to give you."

I sigh deeply, "Uh, ok. What time should I come in?"

"Does today at one o'clock work for you?"

"Yeah, that works. See you then."

"Yes, see you then. And if you could bring Lyric I would love to meet the little guy. Thank you."

We hang up and I look at Allison. "That was Jacquelyn's attorney. She wants me to come in at one today. Says she has something for me."

"Ok, I'll stay here with Lyric."

"She asked me to bring him so why don't you come, too."

"Ok. Now," she grabs my arm, wrapping it around me tightly, "where were we?"

I wrap my hand around her left hand, playing with her ring in between my fingers as I kiss her lips.

Lyric is fast asleep in his car seat as we walk into Jacquelyn's attorney's office hand-in-hand.

"Thank you for coming. Laura Stone, you must be Charles and Allison is it? I heard Charles had a new girlfriend." She reaches her hand out to Allison and I.

"Hello, yes, please call me Charlie and this is Allison, my fiancée."

Laura pauses, then smiles sweetly, "Congratulations. Is this the little guy?" She smiles sweetly, whispering once she sees he's asleep.

"This is our little man," I look down, smiling proudly at Lyric.

"He's such a cutie. Thanks for bringing him in. I knew Jacquelyn for years so it's exciting to meet him. Please, have a seat." She motions to the chairs in front of her desk. "So, you're probably wondering why I called you here today."

"Yes, you said you have something for me. What is it?"

"Well," she sighs deeply. "I'm sure you know now that Jacquelyn had no family and her divorce was complete before the unfortunate incident at her home took place. So, with Lyric as her only living family member," she pauses as her lips turn to a small smile, "her entire estate will be transferred to him and I have drawn out a schedule of payments for you to raise him in the manner that she would have, monetarily I mean."

I sit, stunned, "Excuse me?"

Laura laughs, "Her entire estate, totaled at $50 million along with the monthly royalties she receives for her patents, will be transferred to this little guy with you and I as the executors until he turns 18, or an age that we mutually agree upon. Until then, you will receive payments of $80,000 a month in order to raise him in the manner he would have been raised if Jacquelyn was still alive."

I sit back in my chair, running my hands through my hair before looking over to Allison who's sitting wide eyed, staring at Laura, then me, then Lyric. Both her and I are speechless.

Laura laughs, "I know this is a lot to take in, but I know this is what Jacquelyn would have wanted. She wanted to be a mom more than anything and after seeing this little guy, I know she's smiling down, knowing that he's being fully taken care of."

I grab Allison's hand before looking up to her as my lips tilt up into a small smile. Looking to Allison I say, "We love this little guy more than anything in the world," then I look back to Laura, "Wow, this is just amazing. I promise you we'll do our best to give him the best life he could ever imagine. Thank you for this."

"It's my pleasure. We have a ton of paperwork we will need you to fill out and once we handle the sale of her home we can add that into everything as well. I have your first check made out here. It's for two million to get you started, then your $80,000 will start next month."

She reaches in a drawer and hands me an envelope. I grab it, not being able to hide the fact that I'm shaking.

Laura smiles, "I'll let you get this little guy back home. It was great meeting you both. My assistant will give you all of the paperwork, please send it back to us as soon as you can."

She escorts us out of her office and Allison and I are quiet until we get back in the car.

I go to start the car and pause, looking over at Allison who's still silent. "Well…" I pause, smiling at her.

We both break out laughing as the shock of the moment washes over us and reality hits.

"Did she really say $50 million?" Allison asks.

"Yup, she did. Can you believe it?" I lean over, kissing her before turning on the car and pulling out of the parking spot.

Twenty-Four

Charlie

Allison and I head to Vacaville early in the morning for the annual Fiesta Days Parade. I'm so excited to bring my son to his first parade. Yeah, I know he's only a few weeks old but I don't care. It's been years since I've been to the parade and the thought of reliving some of my greatest childhood memories have filled me with so much hope for the future.

We are meeting Jason and Jen who have a truck set up backwards along the parade route so we can see the parade from a higher point. Allison grew up in San Francisco so this whole small-town parade thing is something that she's never experienced.

We park a few blocks away and walk through the crowds to Merchant Street where the almost mile-long parade route runs as hundreds of people line the streets, waiting patiently for the parade to begin. Allison smiles as she watches all of the kids playing while they wait for the parade to begin.

Jen spots us as we approach and runs to give us a hug. "I'm so glad you guys could make it. Let me see this little man." She moves in front of the stroller. "Ah, he's gotten so big already. Come on, I want to hold this precious baby."

She walks us back to where they're set up and reaches down to grab Lyric from the stroller.

Jason's mom beams from ear to ear saying, "Oh, Charlie. He's precious. Congratulations you two." She gives both Allison and I a hug before stealing Lyric from Jen to hold him close.

I smile proudly, wrapping my arm around Allison as a C5 Air Force jet flies over signally the start of the parade. I can't help but have my eyes tear up at the thought of being here, back in Vacaville with my own family now.

I kiss Allison on the head as we set up our seats and enjoy the almost two-hour long parade.

Afterwards we all go to Jason's parents house for a barbeque. The day is going perfectly and I couldn't be happier.

I have something I want to show Allison before it gets too dark so we say our goodbyes and head out.

I drive through Vacaville out to the country, smiling about what I'm about to show Allison.

She looks around smiling, "I know that little boy grin you have on your face. Where are you taking me?"

I wink at her, "You'll see," as I turn up the radio smiling at the irony of *My Town* by Montgomery Gentry playing.

We pull up to a small country property and I smile to Allison, not able to hide my excitement. I turn to Lyric to see he's fast asleep. Pulling my finger to my mouth, I whisper, "Shhhhh," then tilt my head to the side motioning to quietly get out of the car.

Allison laughs, not sure what I'm up to but gets out of the car and follows me to the front where I grip both of her hands in mine and smile sweetly.

"Allison," I look to the house then back to her. "This is my childhood home. I grew up here."

Allison gasps, smiling as she looks at me and then the house.

"I haven't been back here since I moved in with Jason after my parents passed. I couldn't get rid of it though so I've had a property management company take care of it ever since. The rent I got on it originally just barely covered the mortgage so besides annual phone calls and little things here and there I never thought about it. Until the other day when the management company called to tell me the renters were moving out and it was empty." I pause, leaning down to look straight into her eyes.

"Let's move here." I pause again to gauge her reaction before repeating myself. "Allison, let's raise our son here, in Vacaville. We have enough money now to where we can tear it down and build our dream home. And we can build you a separate building for your own photography studio. And you can live your dream, being an amazing photographer who never has to worry about money so you can shoot only the things you want to. We have five acres. Look, the property goes from here to there." I point at the fence lining the property. "Lyric can play outside anytime he wants when he gets older. I can teach him to throw a ball and ride a bike at the same place I learned how. And Vacaville is such a great community to raise a family in. You saw for yourself today. There are tons of things like that. And I've always wanted to teach kids to play the guitar. Jen said she could set me up to volunteer in the schools here within their music department. She said they're lacking big time with funding so it's perfect. And, I already looked into it, there's a CrossFit Vacaville here…" I say the last line in a sweet enticing voice.

Allison sits silent with no expression on her face. I tense up, afraid of her silence. "What do you think?"

"No," Allison looks down.

I frown, "But Allison…"

"No, Charlie. We can't tear down your childhood home…" She pauses smiling sweetly looking up at me. "We can remodel if you want but I wouldn't dream to tear down any memory of your childhood."

My face explodes with excitement as I wrap my arms around Allison, swinging her around before placing my hands on either side of her face whispering, "I love you, Allison," before I kiss her softly.

We're back home getting ready for bed. I turn to Allison, "I just have to do one thing then I'll be in for bed," I say as I kiss Allison's head.

Allison walks into the bedroom as I sit at the kitchen bar pulling a check out of my wallet. It's a cashier's check for $825,000.

I grab a notepad and an envelope addressing it to Detective O'Brien. Inside the letter I write:

Turns out we did inherit her money. Now go save your girl.

Love,
Mr. Ashley

About the Author

Lauren Runow is a lover of music and songs that speak to her or make her dance. She is a graduate from the Academy of Art in San Francisco and lives in Northern California with her husband and two wild and crazy boys. If she's not at her local CrossFit or working on the community magazine her husband and her publish together, she's at the baseball field with her boys or taking them to the skatepark.

Her only vice is coffee and she swears it makes her a better mom!

Sign up for her newsletter through her website at www.LaurenRunow.com to keep up to date about new releases.

She'd love to hear your comments and feedback. Please take the time to leave a review on Goodreads, Amazon, iBooks or wherever you purchased *Rewritten*.

You can also stay in touch through the social media links below.

www.facebook.com/laurenjrunow

www.twitter.com/LaurenRunow

www.instagram.com/lrunow

www.goodreads.com/author/show/14168280.Lauren_Runow

Playlist for *Rewritten*

- *Up All Night* by Unwritten Law
(Charlie plays this on the way to the hospital to see Jacquelyn for the first time.)

- *Pain* by Three Days Grace
(Charlie stops his workout, contemplating the lyrics to this song.)

- *Love Love Love* by Unwritten Law
(Charlie plays this for Allison when he picks her up from the airport.)

- Beethoven *Symphony No.3 Eroica*
(Charlie plays this the first time him and Allison are back together while they make love.)

- *Waste My Time* by Saint Asonia
(Charlie plays this song for Allison saying it reminds him of himself and how he feels about her.)

- *We Found Love* by Rihanna
(Paul and Nichole dance to this at the club.)

- *Casual Sex* by My Darkest Days
(Nichole sends this song to Paul when they are discussing their relationship status.)
- *Savior* by Rise Against
(After Charlie walks in on Allison and Alex kissing this song plays on the radio. The same song that they first discussed at the coffee shop.)

- *Bad Girlfriend* by Theory of a Deadman
(This song plays at CrossFit when Nichole joins them for the first time on New Years day.)

- *In Da Club* by 50 Cent play

Riot by Three Days Grace

(These are the songs Andy plays at CrossFit on Charlie's birthday.)

For Charlie's birthday scene Allison plays these songs through his earphones.

- *Love Love Love* by Unwritten Law
- *Elva* by Unwritten Law
- *Because of You* by Unwritten Law
- *I Like the Way* by Unwritten Law
- *Rest of My Life* by Unwritten Law

- *Marry Me* by Train

(Plays when Charlie and Allison bring Lyric home from the hospital.)

- *Starships and Apocalypse* by Unwritten Law

(The song that plays at the Unwritten Law concert.)

- *Rest of My Life* by Unwritten Law

(Charlie sings this to Allison when he proposes on stage.)

- *My Town* by Montgomery Gentry

(When Charlie is taking Allison to his childhood home this song comes on the radio.)

Acknowledgements

I can't begin to explain how grateful I am for everyone who has helped make my dreams come true. First and foremost, I'd like to thank my husband Chris who has been so supportive through this entire process and put up with me sitting every night with my computer on my lap or a book in my hand. He's even worked hard at trying to give me material to write about. I am forever grateful for his love and companionship.

Of course, I'd like to thank my best friend Sonia Aguero who has been there since day one of my journey, giving me her ideas, her feedback and of course just moral support. You can thank her for Paul, a name near and dear to her heart with the same dimples to match.

Thank you to my beta readers, Lacy Pryde, Angie Bates, Michelle Strand, Amy Gentili and Leah Purnell for all of your feedback and help making *Rewritten* what it is today.

Entering the world as an author has introduced me to some amazing people who I am forever grateful for, one of them being the amazing author, Jeannine Colette. Her first book, *Pure Abandon*, came out two months before mine and I have no clue what I would have done without her guidance. Her next book, *Reckless Abandon*, just came out and I highly recommend them both!

To my first official fans and creators of my street team, Lauren's Law Breakers, on Facebook, I'd like to thank Giovanna Bovenzi Cruz, Aubrie Brown and Laurie Breitsprecher for their countless hours of promoting me and *Unwritten* on multiple pages through Facebook and Instagram. I can't begin to tell you guys how much I appreciate everything you have done.

My dreams would not have come true without the help of Autumn Hull with Wordsmith Publicity and all of the bloggers who helped spread the word about *Unwritten* by posting cover reveals, teasers and writing reviews. Bloggers are such a huge part of the book world and us writers would be nothing without them so thank you!

Last, but definitely not least, I'd like to thank all the readers out there. An author would be nobody without their readers and I can't tell you what it does to a writer, especially a new one, when someone you don't know reaches out to you to tell you how much they loved your book. It seriously brings tears to my eyes every time I read your emails or posts. From the bottom of my heart, thank you!